w.erlwilson.net or on

...erlwilsonauthr.

Also by Teri Wilson

His Ballerina Bride
The Princess Problem
It Started with a Diamond
Unmasking Juliet
Unleashing Mr. Darcy

Discover more at millsandboon.co.uk

THE BALLERINA'S SECRET

TERI WILSON

MILLS & BOON

First Published in Great Britain 2018
by Mills & Boon, an imprint of HarperCollins*Publishers*
1 London Bridge Street, London, SE1 9GF

The Ballerina's Secret © 2018 Teri Wilson

ISBN: 978-0-263-26505-7

38-0618

MIX
Paper from
responsible sources
FSC™ C007454

This book is produced from independently certified FSC™ paper to ensure responsible forest management.

For more information visit: www.harpercollins.co.uk/green

Printed and bound in Spain
by CPI, Barcelona

For Julia, Karen, Holly and Laird Joanna Macpherson,
the lady laird of Attadale and Attadale Gardens
in the Scottish Highlands, where I wrote the
first four chapters of this book.
I can't wait to go back.

Chapter One

The 66th Street station hummed with music on Monday afternoon. Tessa couldn't hear it, but she could feel the notes vibrating beneath her feet, ever so softly, like a whispered invitation to dance.

It had been a long time since Tessa had actually heard music, or anything else. Over a year. She no longer missed the bustle of crowds, the whoosh of trains or the collective rustling of the morning *Times* in the underground, but thirteen months hadn't been long enough to shake the memory of music echoing off the tile mosaics. Sometimes she still dropped a dollar or two in the occasional violin or guitar case propped open on the gritty concrete floor. The street musician would usually smile in gratitude, and Tessa would smile back.

Then she'd stand and watch the bow slide quietly over the violin strings until the silence grew painful.

Today, the music found her before she even spotted the elderly man wearing a bow tie and fedora, playing the trumpet beside one of the rust-colored pillars on the platform. Before she felt the hum beneath the soles of her shoes. It reached her first by sight. Specifically, by way of the twitch of her dog's ears.

Mr. B loved music. As a hearing-assistance dog, he'd been trained to alert her to specific sounds—the telephone, the alarm clock, people calling her name—but recognizing music wasn't part of his repertoire. Not intentionally, anyway. As best she could tell, he just enjoyed it.

Oh, the irony.

The ground rumbled underfoot as Tessa followed the little dog down the steps and into the station. She'd missed the uptown 1 train by mere minutes, if the near-empty platform was any indication. Other than the trumpet player, she and Mr. B were alone. Tessa gave him a little more slack on his leash, and he trotted straight toward the musician. A jazz player, if she had to venture a guess. He just had that look about him. Maybe it was the bow tie. Or possibly his black-and-white spectator shoes.

She'd worn shoes just like them once—last year, when the Wilde School of Dance had performed a Gershwin tribute. The curtain had gone up on an opening number to *Rhapsody in Blue*, with sultry movements, which were more reminiscent of Bob Fosse than classical ballet. It had been a novelty, wearing something other than pointe shoes. Tessa's feet had been grateful for the respite, even though she was back *en pointe* before the third interlude. Not that she'd minded, really.

Tessa loved pointe shoes. She always had. Some of her earliest memories were made up of watching dancers' pointed feet in the mirrored walls of her mother's dance school while she played in the corner. Dance was in her blood. There had never been any question of whether or not she would take ballet class. Ballet was her destiny, and she'd loved it since the beginning. The moment her hand touched a ballet barre for the first time, she'd been hooked.

She fell for dance. Fast. Hard. As abhorrent as she now found that analogy, it fitted.

Then thirteen months ago, she'd fallen again. For real, this time. In a way, she was still falling. Day after day. And night after night, in her dreams.

She swallowed and blinked hard against the memories. She shouldn't be thinking about her accident. Not now, over a year later, when she'd finally mustered enough courage to put herself out there and go after what she wanted.

When she opened her eyes, she found the trumpet player watching her as he blew into his horn. His eyes were kind, like a grandfather's. This close, she could see the frayed edges of his bow tie and the threadbare spots on the elbows of his suit jacket. She wondered what song he was playing as she reached into her purse for a dollar bill.

She bent down and tossed it into the bucket at his

feet, and when she stood up, she realized a small crowd had gathered. Commuters. Businessmen carrying briefcases. Women in sleek suits. And off to the side, a man with soulful blue eyes and the bone structure of a Michelangelo sculpture. A bit on the intense side. He looked angry, actually. Like a character from a Brontë novel. Heathcliff with a big, fat chip on his shoulder.

And he had an interesting scar next to the corner of his mouth, which enhanced his chiseled features in a way. It made him look less perfect, more human.

An artist of some sort. Tessa would have bet money on it.

But what was she doing staring at a total stranger? Especially one who looked as though he wanted to snatch the trumpet right out of the trumpet player's hands and break it in two over his knee?

The poor old man. She reached into her bag for another dollar and couldn't help noticing Heathcliff's exaggerated eyeroll as she dropped it into the bucket. He shook his head and glared at her.

What a jerk.

Mr. B's leash suddenly went taut in her hands, and Tessa looked down to find the dog standing at attention, staring in the direction of the platform. *The subway car is coming.*

After a year, she could read the dog's body language better than she could read most humans' lips. At home, one nudge of a paw meant a knock on the front door. Two nudges indicated her cell phone had gone off. Repeated face licking first thing in the morning meant rise and shine.

In public, Mr. B's cues were more subtle. He hadn't actually been trained to alert to specific sounds out in the world. But his reactions—even the tiny ones, such as a swivel of his fox-like head or a twitch of his plumed ears—spoke volumes. With Mr. B at the end of his leash, Tessa felt more aware of her environment. Safer somehow.

Inasmuch as Tessa felt safe these days.

She boarded the train, managed to find a spot with a clear, unencumbered view of the digital display of the scheduled stops and tried not to dwell on the fact that the most significant relationship in her life was with a dog. No, that wasn't quite true. Dance had come first. Ballet was the love of her life. The source of her greatest joy, and as fate would have it, her most profound pain. In short, her feelings for dance were complicated.

Which was exactly how people with normal social lives labeled relationships with other actual humans on Facebook. Perfect.

Tessa sighed. She didn't want to think about her relationships, or lack thereof, at the moment. If things had been different, she'd be married to Owen right now. She'd be a wife. Possibly even a mother. Maybe someday she still would.

Then again, maybe not.

There would be time for such things later, when her energy wasn't one hundred percent devoted to rebuilding her career. Love, even friendship. Those things could wait. Couldn't they?

Besides, she wasn't technically a hermit or anything. She taught six classes a week at her mother's dance

school. Granted, most of her students were four-, five-
and six-year-olds. But they were living, breathing people,
with whom she interacted on a daily basis.

Plus she had dancer friends. Sort of. Violet was her
friend at least. The two of them had been auditioning
alongside one another for years. Long enough to give
up any notions of one day becoming primas, or even
making it as far as soloist. Which was fine, really. Tessa
just wanted to dance. She just had to find someone who
would give her a chance.

Keeping up was difficult enough when she could no
longer hear the music. She would be grateful for even
the smallest moment onstage, even if that moment was
spent in the shadows of other dancers. *Better* dancers.

She knew that was a difficult thing for other people,
hearing-people especially, to understand. Which was
why she didn't bother trying to explain it to anyone.
Even her own family didn't seem to get it.

She gave her dog a little squeeze. "It's better this
way, right, Mr. B? Just you and me."

Mr. B craned his neck and gave her a dainty lick on
her cheek.

"Right," she whispered, but couldn't seem to shake
her air of melancholy.

She shouldn't have stopped to watch the trumpet
player in the station. Being unable to hear a melody
she could so clearly see in the movement of a musician's nimble fingers, in the creased concentration of
his brow, had a way of making her more acutely aware
of all she'd lost. And she didn't like to dwell on every-

thing that had slipped through her fingers. Her mother spent enough time doing that on her behalf.

She unzipped her dance tote and pulled out a canvas drawstring bag from Freed of London. She normally didn't splurge on such extravagant pointe shoes. Her shoes didn't matter much when she was teaching little girls how to *plié* all day long. Sometimes she went as long as a week without even dancing *en pointe*.

Then again, this was no ordinary week. The Manhattan Ballet was holding auditions for the next three days, in preparation for a brand-new ballet. Not just any ballet, but an original piece, choreographed by the legendary dancer-turned-choreographer Alexei Ivanov, the biggest dance star to come out of Russia since Mikhail Baryshnikov. He'd only been choreographing for two years, and already critics were comparing him to George Balanchine.

And he was coming here. To Manhattan. Just a few subway stops away from the very studio where Tessa had been dancing since she was three years old.

Ivanov was the reason for the new shoes. Tessa knew her chances of being selected for one of his ballets were slim to none. But she couldn't give up. What kind of dancer would she be if she didn't even try?

The kind of dancer who no longer performed, but only taught classes. That's what kind.

She didn't want to be that kind of dancer. Not anymore. The odds were stacked against her, but she couldn't give up.

Not yet.

She pulled her sewing kit out of the side pocket of

her dance bag and managed to get the needle properly threaded on the first try, despite the jostling of the subway car. She'd sewn ribbons on so many pointe shoes that she could probably do it in her sleep. She might have even done just that a few times during *Nutcracker* season, when back-to-back performances at the Wilde School left the dancers so exhausted, they could barely hold their heads up.

Playing seamstress on a moving train, before the car lurched into her station, would be no problem. With the chore behind her, once she got home, she could ice her feet, take an Epsom-salt bath and head straight to bed.

Because, again, who needs social interaction?

Enough with the self-pity. Tomorrow was important enough that the company dancers at the Manhattan Ballet were probably all planning to get to bed early, too. Even Chance Gabel. Granted, the bed he planned on climbing into likely wasn't his. But still.

Needle threaded, she anchored it into the cuff of her sweater while she untied the drawstring of the slender bag containing her new shoes. She pulled one out, along with a carefully spooled coil of pale pink ribbon. As she positioned the edge of the ribbon alongside the outer seam of the shoes, Mr. B pawed at her hand.

The shoe fell into her lap. Tessa looked up but didn't notice anything out of the ordinary.

"What is it?" she mouthed.

The little dog cocked his head and swiveled his russet ears forward. If she hadn't known better, she would have thought he was trying to alert her to a sound. Some unheard melody that was calling her name.

She glanced at the pregnant woman, who was sitting opposite her, and the pair of Wall Street types, who were standing near the door. No one seemed alarmed, which meant the fire alarm hadn't gone off or anything.

Tessa ran a soothing hand over Mr. B's narrow back. Maybe he was tired. She'd leave him at home tomorrow. She obviously wouldn't be able to drag him along on her audition. The last thing she wanted was to draw more attention to her hearing loss.

But that was okay. She could handle a day in the city without him. She'd have to. It wasn't as though she had a choice in the matter.

She'd be just fine on her own. In her quiet little world. Alone.

Wasn't she always?

Before he even set foot in the subway station, Julian had been less than thrilled by his present circumstances—those circumstances being his growing need for a source of income, despite his fervent lack of interest in leaving his uptown apartment. He'd also just suffered the humiliation of his first job interview in a decade.

Not an interview, technically. Worse. An audition.

For a gig he didn't even want.

The job started tomorrow, and he still didn't know if he'd gotten it. But he would. Chance would see to it that he did, and then, as much as he dreaded the idea, Julian would have no choice but to give it a shot.

Not that he had anything against working. He preferred it, actually, to the nothingness that had slowly taken over his days. He'd just thought that when he finally reached the point where the money from his glory days ran dry, he'd do something else. Anything other than music.

Stumbling upon the trumpet player had nudged Julian's irritation firmly into *pissed* territory. It was a territory he knew, like a favorite song. He spent a lot of time being pissed lately. A couple of years, in fact. But it was better than the alternative. Julian much preferred being thought of as a bitter, cranky prick than as an object of pity. And if no one ever thought of him at all anymore, all the better.

He cursed himself for letting the trumpet player get to him as he climbed on the 1 train. The guy was just an old man. A nobody.

A nobody who can still play the horn.

Right.

He sank into the last open seat in the subway car, which happened to be directly behind the woman who'd dropped a dollar in the old man's bucket. No, not one dollar. Two. And unless Julian had been imagining things, she'd only pulled out the second dollar bill after she'd noticed his disapproval of the musician's performance.

"He wasn't that good, you know." Julian aimed his comment at the back of her head.

Hers was a quite lovely head, actually. Piled with waves of strawberry blond hair, pinned up to expose the curve of her graceful neck. She was pretty. There was something poetic about the way she moved. Lyrical, almost. He'd noticed it straightaway on the train platform. And Julian wasn't prone to noticing such things lately.

His gaze lingered for a moment on a silky, wayward curl winding its way down her back, and he suppressed the urge to twirl it around one of his fingers.

God, what was wrong with him? Had he been shut up in his penthouse for so long that he'd forgotten the rules of simple social interaction? Yeah. He supposed he had.

He cleared his throat and spoke to her again. "I mean, it was nice of you to tip the man. Very nice. All the same, his sense of rhythm was severely lacking."

Why, oh, why was he explaining himself to a woman he didn't even know? A woman who didn't care to know him, apparently.

She didn't budge. She just sat, staring down at something in her lap, while her dog fixed its gaze at Julian over her shoulder. Cute little dog. Copper and white, with plumed ears that seemed almost comically large in proportion to its dainty head. The dog blinked at Julian, cocked its head and swiveled its huge ears forward so they looked even bigger.

"Anyway." Julian sighed. "Like I said, it was nice of you to help the guy out."

He waited a beat, and when she didn't respond— *again*—he turned back around. The two of them spent the rest of their journey back-to-back, mere inches apart.

In silence.

Chapter Two

The sound erupted at rehearsal the next day, and it was nothing like Tessa remembered.

She remembered soft, lilting melodies. The winsome whisper of violins. She remembered the patter of balletic feet and the rhythm of her own labored breath during allegro work at center. In, out. In, out. In, out.

She remembered what the swish of a velvet curtain sounded like on recital night, the deafening roar of a standing ovation and the way roses being tossed onto a stage floor sounded so much like heavy snowfall against a windowpane.

And she remembered music. Of course she did. Even now, she could still hum every theatrical flourish of the *Swan Lake* score from memory. Sometimes she thought she heard songs in her sleep—adagio dreams on good nights and jarring Stravinsky nightmares more often than she cared to admit.

Why shouldn't her subconscious cling to the songs of her youth? Why wouldn't her dreams be set to music? Since the moment she'd slipped on her first pair of ballet slippers, Tessa's life had become a dance. It still was, long after she'd stopped hearing the music.

She could hear it now, though. She didn't know how or why, but she could. Music like nothing that had touched her ears before. Jarring. Bigger than a symphony. Bigger than sound itself. She *felt* it, too, much like she always did, but without an ounce of the concentration it normally took. The notes rose up from the wooden planks of the rehearsal room floor, hummed through the soles of her pointe shoes and into her body like an electrical current. She felt alive with it, almost manic.

Maybe she was crazy. Maybe she'd pulled a Natalie Portman and gone full-on *Black Swan* nuts. God, she hoped not. She'd lost enough since the accident, without adding her sanity to the list.

What in the world was happening, though? Could she be cured? Was it possible for an injury like hers to reverse itself?

Possibly.

The doctors had told her this could happen. But so much time had passed that she'd given up on ever hearing again. She'd made peace with the silence.

The noise in her head was anything but peaceful. She couldn't focus on what her body was doing. She could barely hear herself think.

Tessa felt a tap on her shoulder as she fell out of a

turn. Her legs were moving far too quickly. She could see the other dancers out of the corner of her eye, each with a number pinned to the back of her leotard, just like Tessa. *Unlike* Tessa, they moved in perfect unison. It was mortifying. Tessa spent extra hours in the classroom at the Wilde School of Dance every night to guard against this very thing. She squeezed in extra practice whenever she could. Perfection would never be within her reach. Other girls might have higher arabesques or nicer feet, but Tessa was determined to keep time with the music as well as, or better than, all of them.

It was just so hard to concentrate with the sudden commotion in her head. She'd wished for her hearing to come back for thirteen long months, but she'd never imagined how overwhelming it would be. Or frightening. She wasn't even sure it was real.

Why did it have to happen now, in the middle of her audition? Why was she losing her mind today of all days? She stumbled to a stop and found the company ballet mistress, Madame Daria, standing directly in front of her. Frowning.

"Number twenty-eight?" She stared at Tessa.

Tessa nodded. The number twenty-eight had indeed been assigned to her when she'd shown up bright and early for auditions. It was to be her number for the full three days of tryouts.

If she lasted that long.

"You're off. Count." Madame Daria ticked off her fingers. "Five, six, seven, eight."

Beyond her gesturing hands, her mouth moved. A

fuzzy, indecipherable sound came out of it. Tessa had to read the woman's lips, just she as always did.

She nodded and wiped the sweat from her brow. "Yes, ma'am. I've got it."

This was getting weirder by the minute. She could hear, but nothing sounded right. Everything was too loud, too confusing. Too much.

She wanted to clamp her hands over her ears. Instead, she readied herself to begin again at the next eight count, but Madame Daria's hands abruptly clapped together, and suddenly the music stopped. Tessa's ears rang with melodic echoes.

Thank God. She needed a minute to regroup. She tried inhaling a few deep yoga breaths, and thankfully, everything grew quiet once again. With any luck, it would stay that way.

Still. Silent. Normal.

The other dancers paced or bent over with their hands on their knees, catching their breath, eyes flitting to the studio door in anticipation. Tessa's heart skittered, and she pressed the heel of her hand against her breastbone. This was it. The moment they'd all been waiting for. The arrival of the great Ivanov, the man who could—and often did—make or break a dancer's career on a whim.

And Tessa had just fallen out of a simple *piqué* turn.

Plus, she was suddenly hearing things. Marvelous.

The dancers rearranged themselves—company members near the front, and those who were auditioning crammed in the back of the room. It was less than ideal for Tessa, more difficult to read lips from a distance.

She could have asked to move closer to the front, but she didn't dare. She'd never once asked for special treatment, and she certainly wasn't going to start now.

She fell in line with the others and leaned against the barre beside Violet.

"Are you okay?" Violet pinned back a wisp of hair that had escaped from her ballerina bun.

Tessa shrugged and did her best to feign nonchalance. "Just a little off today. I'll get it together."

"Good." Violet gave her a firm nod, designed, no doubt, to remind her of the importance of the occasion. As if Tessa could forget.

For a moment, she thought about confiding in Violet. But what could she possibly say? She wasn't even sure what was happening herself.

Besides, there was no time. If things didn't go back to normal, she could always talk to Violet after the audition. Then she would make a beeline to her doctor's office.

For now, Tessa scanned the mirrored walls, searching for the best possible angle. She'd become an expert at using the mirrors to her advantage. Out of necessity, of course.

She'd learned to rely almost solely on her sight. As her gaze swept the room, she tried to remember every detail about the space. Until her gaze snagged on the vaguely familiar, scowling man sitting at the piano in the corner.

Him.

She blinked a few times, just in case she'd started seeing things in addition to hearing them. But it was most definitely him—the rude man from the subway station—and he was sitting at the company piano.

Tessa frowned. How had she failed to notice the rehearsal pianist? Particularly *this* rehearsal pianist?

Maybe because you were distracted by the full-scale orchestra in your head?

She stared at the piano player and wondered if he could possibly have something to do with what was happening to her. It was an absurd notion. She was experiencing some kind of medical phenomenon, and the pianist was nothing to her. No one.

He was handsome, though. Quite handsome, actually, with that strong chiseled jaw and those piercing blue eyes that seemed bluer than ever in contrast to his dark hair. And then there was the rather intriguing scar that she'd noticed before by the corner of his lips…it drew her gaze straight to his mouth. His perfectly shaped, perfectly scowling mouth. Why did he seem so annoyed all the time?

Tessa forced her gaze away from his mouth and found him watching her. He lifted a single, accusatory brow, which probably meant he recognized her as the horrible ballerina who'd dared to dance off beat with his playing. Tessa promptly looked away.

She needed to pay attention to the ballet mistress, not the rehearsal pianist.

"Dancers, your attention, please." Madam Daria clasped her hands in front of her as her gaze swept the room. The *front* of the room, technically. The ones who mattered most.

Even the company members were being forced to

audition for Ivanov, though. Technically, no one was safe. The auditioning dancers weren't stars, though. Not like the company members. But that was fine. Tessa was lucky she could still dance at all. And maybe, just maybe, since she was a nobody, the ballet mistress had already forgotten she'd fallen out of her turn.

There were advantages to being invisible.

Daria gestured to the man standing beside her. "Please join me in welcoming Alexei Ivanov. As all of you know, we're honored to have him as the guest choreographer for the Manhattan Ballet's opening program this season. He's agreed to make a new ballet especially for us, which you will begin learning today. Three days from now, twenty of you will be cast in this ballet…if you're lucky."

Tessa clapped along with the rest of the dancers. She didn't realize her gaze had drifted back to the rehearsal pianist until she found him glaring at her. Again. Maybe she wasn't so invisible after all.

Her face grew hot.

Pay attention.

Could this day get any worse? Or more strange, for that matter?

"Everyone take a break. Get a drink of water, but stay warmed up. Be back in your places, ready to go, in exactly ten minutes."

So the great Ivanov didn't plan on deigning to speak a word to them? Fine. Tessa actually preferred it that way. The less talking, the better.

"Auditioning dancers will be up first." Daria's gaze

zeroed in on Tessa. Great. Her mistake hadn't been forgotten after all. "The new ballet begins with a large group number, and it's very intricate. You all need to be on your A-game. Let's not waste Mr. Ivanov's time."

Tessa swallowed around the lump in her throat, and like clockwork, her mother's voice echoed in her consciousness.

You're a great teacher, Tessa. The children love you, and the Wilde School of Dance is your home. There will always be a place for you here. It's easier this way.

Tessa didn't want to take the easy way out. She didn't want to be a ballet teacher for the rest of her life. Teaching would mean giving up. Teaching would mean the accident had stolen the one thing she'd loved most. Ballet.

She wanted to dance. Not teach.

Dance.

Dance was all she had left. It was all she'd ever wanted, and she'd worked too hard, for too long, to mess everything up now.

She'd do better. She just had to figure out a way to ignore the racket in her head.

She sneaked another glance at the piano player, and sure enough, the noise she heard matched the movement of his elegant hands as they moved across the keys in a series of warm-up scales. He had such lovely hands. They danced across the piano keys with a grace that made her chest ache.

Or maybe that ache was just the realization that this strange man's music had been the first thing she'd heard in over a year.

* * *

Don't ogle the dancers.

It had been the main rule Julian had been given when Chance passed along the job offer. The only rule, in fact. And therefore, the most important.

"No problem," he'd said.

And he'd meant it. Julian had known Chance long enough to lose any romantic notions he might have had about the ballet world. In the ten years they'd been friends, Julian could count on one hand the number of times Chance hadn't been a foul, sweaty mess. Ballet wasn't art. It was work. Messy, fanatic work.

Besides, Julian had no interest in a roomful of underfed women who considered him invisible. He had no interest in being here at all, frankly.

He should have saved his money. He should have planned or invested. Something. Anything. He'd had a good run. A stellar run, actually. How could he have possibly known it wouldn't last?

He wasn't even a piano player, for crying out loud. He'd told Chance as much. What was it that Chance had said in response? *We don't need Mozart. We need a body. You're good enough.*

Good enough.

Oh, how the mighty had fallen.

He sighed, crossed his arms and waited for *Madame* Daria to finish her big speech. She'd actually asked him to call her that. Madame. Like they were in nineteenth-century France or something. Not happening.

She droned on about the new choreographer, some Russian hotshot. Julian glanced at his watch. He'd been on the job for less than an hour, and already he was bored out of his mind. This whole thing had been a mistake. If he managed to get through the day without falling asleep and knocking his head on the piano keys, it would be a miracle.

Five more hours. That's all.

He could last five hours. Then when it was over, he'd quit. Chance would understand. Probably. If he didn't, too damn bad.

Julian sighed. Then he looked up and found one of the dancers staring at him. The only one who'd managed to capture his attention in the entire hour and a half he'd been banging away on the Steinway. The dancer who'd made the mistake.

The girl from the train.

Truth be told, he'd noticed her even before she'd wobbled out of her turn. Before he'd even recognized her. He couldn't help it. Until his hands had touched the keys, she'd been just another whisper-thin girl in a wraparound leotard and tights.

But then he'd begun to play, and she'd transformed right before his eyes. One note. That's all it had taken. Her eyes had grown wide, and she'd flung herself into the dance. If Julian hadn't known better, he would have thought she'd never heard music before. Maybe because there was something different about the way she moved. Desperate. Like she was running from a demon.

Madame had been right, though. The girl had been dancing off beat, which should have annoyed him. It didn't. Much to his irritation, he found her intriguing.

Probably because Julian was no stranger to demons himself.

The ballerina's gaze lingered on his lips. Or more probably, his scar.

Of course.

Every muscle in Julian's body tensed as his fascination with her morphed into something closer to disdain. Not that he was surprised. Or even disappointed. He was grateful, actually. He'd learned a long time ago not to mix business with pleasure.

Of course he had no intention of sticking to this gig, but still. Knowing Chance, he'd probably already bedded the ballerina since he seemed to make it his mission to sleep his way through every ballet school and company in Manhattan. Which made his advice all the more ridiculous.

Don't ogle the dancers.

Right.

Julian wasn't ogling. He absolutely wasn't. If anything, the pretty ballerina was ogling *him*.

Her gaze drifted upward, and their eyes locked. When she realized she'd been caught staring at his scar, her cheeks went pinker than her ballet shoes.

Julian lifted a brow. *Go ahead, sweetheart. Look your fill.*

She looked away, her deepening flush the only evidence of their nonverbal exchange.

Julian sank onto the piano bench and flipped through the sheet music Madame had thrust at him upon his arrival. The score for the audition was Debussy. He was to open with *Rêverie*, which he rather liked. It was a vast improvement over the repetitive chords he'd had to play for the morning barre exercises. Debussy's *Rêverie* had also been the inspiration for the melody of "My Reverie," a favorite of Julian's. He owned recordings of both Sarah Vaughan's and Ella Fitzgerald's renditions. On vinyl.

He let his hands hover over the keys and played the melody silently, in his head, if only to keep from seeking out the interesting ballerina at the back of the room again. Even so, he found himself watching her more often than he cared to admit. It came as a relief when Daria rapped her hand on the piano and ordered him to play. Not asked, ordered.

Julian banged out the opening melody over and over again, in half time, as the dancers learned their parts. After the first fifteen rounds, he could have played the score in his sleep, so he let his gaze wander to the action in the center of the room, while his hands moved by rote. The Russian demonstrated the steps, and the dancers mimicked him. Sometimes he grabbed a foot or an arm and physically moved it where he wanted it to go. He did this a lot, actually. There was only one dancer he never touched. Her.

Julian wondered if this was good or bad. Then he wondered why he cared.

On and on, he played, until the sunshine streaming through the windows grew dim and blue shadows stretched across the studio floor. The dancers peeled away leg warmers and layers of clothing, and the air in the room felt heavy and damp. The combination they'd been working on began to take shape. Chance and a few others had long since gone home, but the remaining ballerinas with numbers pinned to their black leotards moved in perfect sync, arms slanted at elegant angles, heads tilted just so.

Except her. Number twenty-eight.

Tessa.

He'd learned her name after all the corrections Daria had barked at her over the course of the day. She wasn't off beat anymore, but she couldn't seem to rein herself in. That was the difference. She danced bigger than everyone else. Bigger than was acceptable, if the dour expression on Daria's face was any indication. But when the Russian watched her, he smiled.

Again, why Julian noticed any of this was a mystery. At any rate, he wasn't ogling. He was simply observing. What was he supposed to do all day? Stare at the black-and-white keys?

He reached the end of the piece, and Daria clapped her hands. "That will be all for today. Tomorrow morning we'll have barre exercises and run through the combination a final time. Then we'll begin the selection process. Good work, everyone." She glanced up and down the row of dancers and nodded, never once letting her gaze rest on Tessa. "You're dismissed."

Julian rearranged the sheet music for whoever took his place tomorrow and situated it on the rack of the Steinway. His hands ached. His back ached. He cursed under his breath, remembering a time when he could play his trumpet for hours, days, weeks at a time without so much as a sore pinky finger. Quite the opposite, in fact. He'd felt loose then. Liquid. Smooth. Like Coltrane.

And now here he was. Broken down after a few hours on a piano bench.

At least he felt something, though. He'd been numb for a while. A long while. He wasn't altogether sure which was worse—the numbness or this new dull ache.

"Mr. Shine." He looked up and found Daria staring down at him, hands planted on her slim hips. Behind her, he could see Tessa sitting alone beneath the barre, untying the ribbons of her pointe shoes. She'd loosened her hair from its ballerina bun, and it fell about her shoulders in lush copper waves. The ache in his hands intensified, and he had the sudden urge to find out what that beautiful hair would feel like sliding through his fingers.

He cleared his throat and damned the reawakening of his senses. "Daria."

She stared daggers at him. "It's *Madame*."

He smiled and said nothing. He was only half paying attention, anyway. Tessa had removed her shoes, revealing her gracefully arched feet. They were flushed. Cherry red. She looked as though she'd been walking barefoot through a field of poppies.

"You were satisfactory today," Daria said primly.

Satisfactory.

Julian suppressed an eyeroll. Other than his short audition the day before, today marked the first time he'd played any sort of music in two years. Two years, one month and sixteen days, to be exact. Not that he was counting. The days somehow counted themselves, no matter how hard he tried to stop keeping track.

Two years. He supposed *satisfactory* wasn't the worst assessment in the world. What had he expected?

He didn't even know, other than he'd thought it would be somewhere besides a ballet studio, where the only people who knew his name were Chance and a task-mistress who barely cleared five feet tall. A taskmistress who clearly expected him to show up again tomorrow.

"I'll expect you at nine o'clock in the morning," she said. "Sharp."

Thanks, but no, thanks.

"Fine." He turned on his heel, telling himself it wasn't too late. He could still get out of this.

Say it. Just say it. I'm not coming back.

But the words stuck in this throat as his footsteps echoed past the empty space where Tessa had been.

Chapter Three

"New pointe shoes?" Tessa's mother, Emily Wilde, eyed the Freed of London bag sticking out of her dance bag.

Ugh, why hadn't she zipped it properly? Never mind, though. She'd done nothing wrong. She didn't have anything to hide.

Other than the weird sounds she'd heard yesterday, obviously. That was a different story, and much more serious than an audition for a part she probably wouldn't even get.

"I'm auditioning for the Manhattan Ballet." Tessa unclipped Mr. B's leash and let him loose in the dance school. He trotted to the dog bed in the corner of the main classroom, spun three circles and then collapsed in a furry little heap.

When Tessa looked up, her mother had already

begun signing. Her hands moved through the air in an alphabetic flurry. "Again? Oh, Tessa."

"Yes, again." She wondered what her mother's voice sounded like now. Emily never talked when she signed, so Tessa couldn't tell if she sounded the same.

Probably not. Nothing sounded like it should. She felt as though she'd woken up a day ago at the bottom of the ocean. Everything sounded muffled. Distorted. Not at all like she remembered.

"I need you to look after Mr. B today, okay?" He'd expressed his displeasure about being left behind the day before by disemboweling a throw pillow. There'd been more feathers on her living room floor than in the first three acts of *Swan Lake*. "And possibly tomorrow."

Her mother's eyebrows shot up. "Tomorrow, too?"

If I last that long. "The cast list goes up tomorrow afternoon."

"I see." Her mom nodded. "And will you be back today in time for the preschool tap class?"

Preschool tap. What on earth would that sound like? Tessa didn't want to know. God help her. "Sorry, I have a doctor's appointment late today. Can we get Chloe to cover it?"

Her sister, Chloe, *should* be the one teaching tap, anyway. She was a Rockette. She lived in tap shoes. But she always had something more pressing to do. More important. It was getting kind of old, truth be told.

"I'll check." Her mother's eyes narrowed. "I didn't realize you'd scheduled a doctor's appointment. Is everything okay?"

Tessa had no idea how to answer that question.

Things were *not* okay, which was why she'd made the appointment to begin with.

But if she was truly getting her hearing back, wouldn't it get better? It had to. She couldn't live like this. She'd rather be deaf.

"Everything's fine." She pasted on a smile.

She'd tell her mom what was going on once she had a handle on things. She couldn't deal with any additional drama. Not when she still had two more days of auditions to get through.

"Good. I'll see you later, then. Don't worry about Mr. B. He loves it here."

As should you.

Emily didn't say so. She didn't have to. Tessa got the message loud and clear.

She wanted too much. She should be happy teaching dance. Which was probably why her mom hadn't even wished her good luck at her audition. She probably hadn't thought to wish her well. She'd just assumed Tessa wouldn't make it. Just like all the other times she'd auditioned in the past year.

Tessa glanced at the clock on the wall above the record player that had been a fixture at the studio since she'd been too little to reach the barre. It was late. She wouldn't have to worry about her audition if she didn't hurry to make the train. She waved goodbye to Mr. B, and left.

While she sat in the subway car, she mentally reviewed the combination Ivanov had taught them the day before. The train made a terrible noise, though. Much louder than the music from Heathcliff's piano.

Heathcliff. She really should stop calling him that, even to herself. Surely the man had a name.

Don't you have more important things to be concerned about?

She did. Namely, the time.

She flew into the Manhattan Ballet studio with only ten minutes to spare. Through the tiny window at the end of the hall, she saw Chance Gabel standing just a little too close to Sabrina Cox, one of the other principal dancers. Neither of them was dancing, or paying the least bit of attention to anyone or anything, other than each other. Which meant rehearsal hadn't started.

Good. She wasn't late.

Yet.

She pushed the door open, intent on getting to her spot and slipping her shoes on as quickly as possible. But instead of darting inside, she crashed into something. Some*one*, technically. The shoes she carried in her arms tumbled to the floor, and she found herself face-to-face with the angry piano player.

Face to chest, actually, as he was a good six or seven inches taller than she was. But unlike the permanent scowl on his face, his chest was rather nice. Firm. Solid beneath her fingertips, which for some ridiculous reason, had lingered there. His T-shirt was even balled in her fists, which she could only assume was a result of her recent mental breakdown.

"I'm sorry." She swallowed. "So sorry."

He looked at her as though she'd materialized out of thin air, which she sort of had, since she'd flown right into the room. He started to say something, but she didn't catch it because her gaze dropped to her hands, still gripping his shirt like he was her own personal, perfectly muscular security blanket.

She ordered her balled fists to let go, and they flagrantly disobeyed. Then, to her even greater mortification, the piano man's musical fingers wrapped around hers and unfastened them for her. As per usual, there was a scowl on his face. Tessa didn't know if it was due to the fact that she'd plowed straight into him, or because it seemed to be his default expression. Resting Heathcliff face.

Oh, God.

She scrambled to the floor to gather her shoes together. Rehearsal was mere seconds away, and she wasn't anywhere near her spot. She felt altogether vulnerable. Exposed. As if every pair of eyes in the room was bearing down on her, but when she glanced up, no one was watching.

Only him.

The dancer, Tessa, was in a panic, and Julian only seemed to be making things worse.

"It's okay," he said. "Rehearsal can't start without the music, and I guess you could say that's me. I'm the music."

He waited for a laugh. Or a smile. Neither was forthcoming. Not even a hint of acknowledgment. Just like on the train.

Okay, then.

He sat back on his heels and watched her gather her things. She might not want to give him the time of day.

Correction—not might. She *clearly* didn't. And while that realization didn't please him in the slightest, he had no desire to see her punished for being tardy. The Russian appeared so full of himself, he'd abhor such a violation. If for some reason he took it in stride—a possibility that seemed slim at best—Madame Daria would never let it slide. Of that, Julian was certain.

Still.

He prickled at being slighted by Tessa. Again. Granted, this was her world, not his. He was in a dance studio, not some smoky blues club in the West Village, where, even now, he could have his pick of women.

Maybe.

Probably.

He had no interest in actually putting that theory to the test. Why he cared at all what the willowy creature who'd practically mowed him down thought of him was a mystery.

Except they'd had something of a moment, hadn't they? A moment when she'd held on to him a little too long, when his heart had beaten a little too hard. It had happened so fast, he would have thought he'd imagined it, if not for the memory of his shirt gathered in her clenched fists. For a second, he'd nearly remembered what it had felt like to belong to someone.

Then he'd come to his senses. He knew nothing about this girl, other than that she was a beautiful dancer. More important, she didn't know the first thing about him.

Now her head was bowed, and Julian couldn't help noticing the lovely curve of her shoulders, the grace of her willowy neck and how very pale and delicate her complexion looked set off by her jet-black leotard.

God, she was gorgeous. Too gorgeous to waste away in the corner of the room, with a number pinned to her back, while Chance preened like a peacock less than three feet away from the mirrored walls. Not that Julian harbored any ill will toward his friend. Chance had gotten him this gig after all. Of course, it wasn't exactly the best gig in the world. Far from it.

But coming here had gotten him off the sofa and out of the house. As pathetic as that sounded, it was progress.

Somewhere in the very near vicinity, a throat cleared. Julian glanced over his shoulder to find Madame Daria looming over him. *Honestly, lady. Give it a rest.*

He rose to his feet as slowly as humanly possible and shot her a lazy grin. "Daria."

Her face grew red. Julian had anticipated an angry reaction, and Madame didn't disappoint. "Mr. Shine, our rehearsal time started three minutes ago. You're holding up the entire audition."

Julian clutched his heart in mock regret. "My sincerest apologies."

She rolled her eyes and waved toward the grand piano with a flourish. "Shall we begin?"

"Absolutely."

She turned on her pink-slippered heel and joined the Russian at the front of the room. Julian's gaze snagged briefly on Chance, who just shook his head in obvious disgust. Julian's only response was a slight shrug of his shoulders before Chance turned away and launched into a grand *tour en l'air*.

Message received. Madame wasn't the object of Chance's derision. Julian himself was.

Don't ogle the dancers.

Right.

He looked down at Tessa, still sitting at his feet, tying satin ribbons around her ankles with trembling fingers.

"Allow me," he murmured and reached for Tessa's elbow to help her up.

She promptly ignored him. Yet again.

He stood there, feeling like an idiot, while she rose gracefully to her feet—unassisted—and walked away from him without so much as a backward glance. He'd been agitated at being ignored the first time but was willing to overlook it. The second time, not so much. He'd basically put his job on the line to buy her a little time. Granted, it was a job he didn't particularly care for. A crap job, really. But Tessa didn't know that, did she?

He stalked toward the piano, all the while reminding himself he had no interest in romantic liaisons. He was a mess. Messed up enough to know better than to become involved with someone. *Any*one, much less a woman who looked right through him.

He'd forgotten himself for a moment—that was all. He wasn't the man he'd been two years ago. Inside or out. A glance in any direction in this mirrored room was all the reminder he needed.

Madame Daria clapped her hands, and Julian dutifully pounded out some Debussy. Row by row, the dancers spun around him until the studio was little more than a dizzying blur of lithe, lean bodies and spinning pink satin. Despite every effort to the contrary, Julian's gaze found Tessa. Time and again. He told himself it was only because Madame kept screaming corrections at her, sometimes quite literally in her face.

He almost believed it.

He wasn't coming back. This time, he meant it. At the end of rehearsal, he took painstaking care to make sure he left the sheet music in the exact right order. Anyone should be able to pick up right where he'd left off. He thought idly for a moment about who that person might be, and then decided he didn't care. What difference did it make?

We don't need Mozart. We need a body.

Right. Well, that body would no longer be his.

"What are you doing?" Chance leaned against the piano and crossed his arms. If Julian had any sentimental attachment to the baby grand, he would have chastised Chance for getting his sweat all over it. Maybe wiped the Steinway down with a towel.

But he didn't. "Packing up. What does it look like I'm doing?"

If Chance realized he'd meant permanently, he didn't bring it up. He grabbed a T-shirt out of the dance bag at his feet and pulled it on, as the last remaining dancers slipped out of the room. "I saw you looking at her, you know. We all did."

A pain shot through Julian's temple. "I don't know what you're talking about."

"Yes, you do. The girl. Number twenty-eight." Chance's tone was altogether too dismissive for Julian's taste. She had a name after all.

"Am I to assume you're talking about Tessa?"

Chance raised a brow. "Ah, so you admit it."

"I admit nothing. Can we not do this?" It was a moot point, anyway. This time tomorrow, he wouldn't be here to stare at Tessa. Or anyone.

"Listen, I know I said not to ogle the dancers. It grates on Madame's nerves. Just try and be a tad more subtle next time, would you?" He shook his head. "Besides, you can do better than a dancer who isn't even part of the company. Two of the soloists asked about you yesterday. I think they know who you are."

Who I am.

Who am I?

It was a question he'd been asking himself on a daily basis since he'd put down his trumpet for the final time. "What have you got against auditioning dancers? You were one yourself a while back."

"Nothing." Chance shrugged. "But if you're going to pick one, at least pick a good one."

Julian tossed the sheet music in a pile on top of the Steinway. "What are you talking about? Are you blind? She's nothing like the other ballerinas."

"Exactly. That's the problem. She's not supposed to stand out. You're not supposed to notice her at all. She's auditioning for the corps. The corps dancers all have one job. The same job. They move in perfect unison. They're background."

"That's a rather harsh description, don't you think?" Julian slung his messenger bag over his shoulder and headed toward the door. He'd spent long enough on this conversation. Too long, actually.

Chance fell in step beside him. "Not harsh. Accurate. She's going to get cut. Mark my words. When your little Tessa stands out, it's because she's screwing up."

His little Tessa. Hardly. He didn't even know why he was having this conversation.

He stalked wordlessly down the hall, hoping against hope Chance would just drop it.

"There she is now," Chance said and pointed at a slender window in one of the smaller studio's doors.

Don't do it. Don't look.

He looked. Because apparently there was some truth to Chance's accusations. Maybe he'd stared. Maybe there'd even been some ogling.

He found her attractive. So what? He was only human. It didn't mean he wanted to pursue anything. It simply meant he was a normal, red-blooded male.

Of course he hadn't felt much like a normal, red-blooded male in a while. A long while. But what he saw when he looked through that window stirred an undeniably primal reaction in him. He had to suppress a groan.

Eyes closed, arms fluttering like a butterfly, Tessa moved across the floor on tiptoe. Like those times she'd been chastised in rehearsal, she moved with complete and utter abandon. Only now, alone in the semidarkened studio, there was no one there to rein her back in. No Russian. No Madame. Just Tessa, dancing for no one but herself. It was one of the most beautiful sights Julian had ever set eyes on.

A strange, dull ache formed in the center of his chest. He felt as though he were witnessing something he shouldn't, some inherently private moment. Maybe it was the way she danced with her eyes closed. Or maybe it was the stillness of the lonely studio. Maybe both. He wasn't sure. All he knew was that every stretch of her arm, every lithe arabesque, seemed to impart a secret. A secret born in pain and longing. She moved with such melancholy grace that it almost hurt to watch.

"Why is she still here?" he asked and wondered if Chance noticed the sudden edge to his voice. God, he hoped not.

"It's something she does." Chance shrugged, seemingly oblivious. "She practices. Pretty much every chance she gets, not that it's doing much good. This is the fourth time she's auditioned."

She practices every chance she gets? After a full day in the studio?

"That doesn't sound like your typical dancer to me." As if Julian actually knew the first thing about ballet.

Chance shook his head. "She'd never work out."

"People improve. New dancers get chosen all the time." Julian lifted a brow. "You did."

"Now you're comparing her to me? I thought you'd barely noticed her." Chance let out a laugh. "She'll never get chosen. She can't handle it. It would be too much work."

Julian watched as she traveled the entire length of the room on her toes, with the tiniest steps imaginable. She looked like she was floating on a cloud. Or through a dream. He swallowed. Hard. "She doesn't strike me as someone who's afraid of hard work."

Chance's eyes narrowed. "You don't know, do you?"

Julian tore his gaze from the window. Finally. "Don't know what?"

"Tessa can't hear. She's deaf."

It took Julian a minute to process what Chance was saying. Even then, it didn't make any sense. "What do you mean she can't hear?"

"She had an accident a year or so ago." *An accident.* Chance dropped his gaze. He knew full well that Julian was no stranger to accidents.

"What kind of accident?"

Chance cleared his throat. "A ballet accident. Her partner dropped her during a lift, and she hit her head. He wasn't just her dance partner either. He was also her fiancé."

Julian thought back to the moment she'd crashed into him before rehearsal, the utterly blank look on her downturned face when he'd told her not to worry and the brush-off she'd given him when he'd tried to help her up. He remembered the way her head hadn't moved at all when he'd spoken to her on the train. She hadn't been slighting him. She'd never heard a word he'd said.

He shook his head. No. It just wasn't possible. "How does she even do it? How does she know what's being said in class? How does she dance?"

"She reads lips, and she counts the beats."

She reads lips.

Without realizing what he was doing, Julian ran his fingertips across his own lower lip. Then he made contact with the scar tissue near the corner of his mouth, and his hand fell away.

He glanced at the window again, even though everything within him told him to turn around. Turn around and walk away. While he still could. None of this was his concern. In the silvery light of the mirrored room, Tessa's eyes fluttered open. Her gaze fixed with his, and Julian knew it was already too late.

Chapter Four

Conductive hearing loss as a result of ossicular chain discontinuity due to head trauma.

Tessa glanced at the words printed on the bright orange sticker on the tab of the file folder in the nurse's hands.

Her diagnosis.

It had taken her doctors—four of them in all, led by Dr. Meryl Spencer, an auditory specialist at Mount Sinai—ten days and a total of three different hearing tests to settle on one. It was really just a fancy way of saying what everyone suspected. When she'd fallen and hit her head, she'd sustained damage to the delicate bones in her middle ear. They were no longer connected properly, which prevented sound from being conducted to her brain. It was impossible to tell the extent of the damage, or whether or not her hearing loss was permanent, until her body healed.

In the words of Dr. Spencer, it was "a waiting game."

So Tessa waited.

And waited.

All in all, she'd been waiting for thirteen months. Thirteen months of adjusting to a life of silence—a life without the sound of laughter or the voices of the people she loved or the Manhattan street noises that Tessa hadn't realized were so ingrained in her consciousness until she no longer heard them. A life without music.

But she'd adjusted. She'd done it. Through it all, she'd never lost the one thing she loved most of all. She'd never lost dance.

Tessa wasn't waiting anymore. She hadn't been waiting for a while now. She was getting on with things. So thirteen months was probably an exaggeration. She wasn't sure when she'd given up the notion that she'd ever hear again, but she most definitely had. What kind of person would hold out hope after all this time?

"The doctor will be with you in just a moment." The nurse offered Tessa a soothing smile and slid the file folder into a plastic chart holder on the door to the exam room.

"Thank you." Tessa nodded.

Once the nurse was gone, Mr. B, who'd accompanied Tessa to the after-hours appointment, relaxed and settled into a comfortable ball. Seconds later, when Dr. Spencer opened the door, the little dog popped back up.

"Hello, Tessa. And hello to you, too, Mr. B. It's good to see you both," the doctor said.

"You, too." Tessa exhaled a calming breath. *Everything's going to be fine. There's a simple explanation for all of this.*

Right. Because traumatic head injuries were so often classified as simple.

That was never the case. Literally never. Not even a year after the fact.

"Thank you for seeing me on such short notice." Tessa shifted, and the paper on the exam table made a terrible, crunching sound. She winced.

Dr. Spencer's brow furrowed, and she pulled an otoscope from the pocket of her white coat. "Your email said you'd been experiencing some auditory symptoms. Why don't you tell me what's going on, and I'll take a look inside your ears?"

Auditory symptoms. What an innocuous way to describe the chaos in her head. "I can hear all of a sudden, but it's not right. The noises are distorted. Too loud. Too…" Too much. Much too much.

The doctor asked her more questions and examined her ears using the otoscope. When she was finished, she slipped the instrument back inside her pocket and smiled. Tessa hadn't seen Dr. Spencer smile much before, if ever. Her bedside manner was usually polite, efficient and a little on the brusque side. Then again, maybe there'd just never been anything about Tessa's case to smile about. Until now.

"It seems as though there's been a change in the connectivity between the bones of your right middle ear. That's the most likely possibility. It's good news, Tessa. Potentially very good news."

Tessa swallowed and glanced down at Mr. B, who was wagging his tail. *Good news.* It didn't feel so good. "But what does it mean, exactly?"

Dr. Spencer nodded, and her smile grew even wider. "It means that the hearing in your right ear is potentially on the road to being restored."

Her right ear only. That explained why she'd felt so lopsided and out of balance. And why she'd fallen out of a *piqué* turn during her audition.

"You don't seem nearly as happy about this development as I'd expected. This is what we've been waiting for, Tessa. To be honest with you, I'd nearly given up on any kind of natural healing of the connectivity in your middle ear. It's been a year."

As if Tessa didn't know the exact date she'd fallen. September 14. She'd never forget.

"It's just nothing like I expected." A siren wailed somewhere outside the building—an ambulance most likely. A migraine began to blossom behind Tessa's right eye. "Everything is so loud. Distorted. Something must be wrong."

She blinked back tears. Mr. B pawed at her foot and gazed up at her, his soft brown eyes wide with worry.

Dr. Spencer scooped the dog into her arms and placed her in Tessa's lap. "I understand your concern, and I promise what you're experiencing is completely normal. Remember how difficult it was to adjust to your hearing loss? It took time and patience. You need to be gentle with yourself now, just as you were before. Hearing has a profound effect on a person's perspective on life. It's time to alter your perspective again."

Alter her perspective. She could do that. She'd done it before, hadn't she? "How so, exactly?"

"The only surefire answer is time. I'm going to give you the same advice I give patients right after they receive cochlear implants. Reduce your amount of external stimuli as much as possible. Take things slow. Stay home so you can get used to the common sounds of everyday life. Eventually, the sound won't be so disorienting for you."

"Stay home," Tessa echoed.

At least she'd already told her mother she couldn't teach tap tonight. If she went straight home after this appointment, she'd have a solid eleven or twelve hours before she had to leave for the final day of auditions in the morning.

She nodded. "Fine. How long are we talking about, exactly?"

Dr. Spencer shrugged. "It varies. It's different for everyone. Once you've gotten reacquainted with the surroundings in your own little world, you can start to venture out of your house. Sometimes it takes months. Most of the time, only a matter of weeks. You used to hear, so the process should go more smoothly for you. I'd say take two to three weeks to yourself before you venture out again."

Two to three *weeks*? Impossible. "But I can't do that. I'm auditioning for the Manhattan Ballet. I have to be in the studio tomorrow."

Dr. Spencer's smile vanished altogether. "Now probably isn't the best time to tackle something new, Tessa."

"I can't drop out midaudition. I might never get this

chance again." She shook her head. No. Just no. She couldn't lose another year of her life. She wouldn't. "Maybe it's not as serious as you think it is. Could this be temporary? Remember the tinnitus I had just a few weeks after the accident? It went away. This could, too, right?"

She was grasping at straws. What's more, she wasn't making sense. What head injury patient with conductive hearing loss complained about her hearing potentially coming back?

Judging from the bewildered look on Dr. Spencer's face, none of them did. Only Tessa. "The tinnitus was indeed temporary, thank goodness. Some patients go their entire lives with ringing in their ears. I was relieved beyond measure when it became clear you wouldn't be one of them."

Tessa swallowed around the lump in her throat. She should be grateful.

And she was. Truly.

She just wished her right ear had waited a day or two before deciding to heal itself, or whatever was going on in there.

Of course, what difference would a day or two have made if she got cast in the new ballet and earned a part in the company? None. Although that possibility was looking less likely by the minute.

"To answer your question, yes. This could only be temporary, too. Head trauma is unpredictable." The doctor reached around Mr. B to give Tessa's hand a squeeze. "I hope it's not. Deep down, I think you hope the same thing."

The doctor was right.

Tessa nodded.

But since the day thirteen months ago, when her partner dropped her at ballet rehearsal, Tessa's hope had taken a serious hit. She wasn't sure how much she had left anymore.

The solution seemed obvious—Tessa was going to have to withdraw from the auditions.

She waited until the next morning to decide, on the off chance that she'd wake up and find that everything had gone back to normal. Normal, meaning silent. She didn't breathe a word about what happened at her doctor's appointment to her mother, or anyone else, for that matter. How silly would it have been to have to go back and explain that she hadn't gotten her hearing back after all?

She was in denial. Clearly. Because when she woke up and turned on the bathroom faucet to brush her teeth, it sounded as though she were standing on the edge of Niagara Falls.

I can't keep going like this and pretending nothing is happening.

She was quitting.

Maybe someday she'd get to audition again, *if* they agreed to give her another chance. Tessa wasn't holding her breath.

She was going to explain to Madame Daria in person, though, just in case it might make a difference next year. Or the year after that. It would be her last trip outside for the next few weeks. Her swan song. Then she'd follow Dr. Spencer's advice and hole herself up until the world made sense again.

Tessa rode the 1 train to the studio, took a deep breath as she walked inside the building and headed straight to the business office. There wasn't a soul in sight through the frosted glass window. She drummed her fingernails on the counter and waited as her gaze snagged on one of the company soloists darting down the hall. Victoria French.

Victoria had danced the lead in the company production of *Giselle* last season. Tessa had watched her breathtaking performance from a balcony seat on opening night. Everyone, Tessa included, expected her to be cast in the lead in the new Ivanov ballet. It was the most coveted role. Not only was it the biggest part, but the costume for the lead ballerina would feature a bodice woven with gemstones from Manhattan's most upscale jeweler, Drake Diamonds.

Victoria was clearly in a hurry but headed toward the dressing rooms, rather than the practice studio. The ribbon on one of her pointe shoes trailed behind her, dragging on the floor. Odd. If Tessa hadn't known better, she would have sworn Victoria had been crying.

She stared after Victoria, until someone else rounded the corner. Not a dancer this time, but him. The piano player.

Before she could look away, he waved. No, not waved. Not exactly.

His fist was closed, and he circled it in the air. Tessa blinked, unsure what to make of the gesture. He repeated it, only this time he clapped first. Two deliberate claps, followed by the fist-circling motion. Then he smiled—his version of a smile at least—just a subtle tug at the corner of his mouth. The corner without the scar.

That's when it hit her. He wasn't waving. He was *signing.*

Her stomach did a little flip. The piano man knew American Sign Language? How was that possible? And how did he even know she was deaf?

Tessa had never come across anyone in ballet circles who knew how to sign. Even Owen had never tried. She'd started signing with her family about six months after her accident, when it seemed as though her hearing loss had come to stay. Other than that, she read lips.

She stared at the piano player, this mysterious man who suddenly seemed far more mysterious than she could have imagined. A lump lodged in her throat for some silly reason.

He made the motion again—two sharp claps and a circled fist—then looked at her expectantly.

Congratulations.

Why on earth would he be congratulating her?

She made a fist, pressed it to her heart and moved it in a circle. *I'm sorry.* Then she shook her head and pointed twice to the sky. *I don't understand.*

His grin widened. Just a bit. And he shrugged. Apparently, she wasn't the only one who didn't understand. Did he know sign language or not?

"Um." She bit her lip, unsure what to say, unsure why he made her so nervous.

Because he knows too much. Because he knows.

Ridiculous. He couldn't possibly know that she'd

suddenly begun to hear things. She didn't even know where that thought had come from. He just had a way of looking at her that her made her feel exposed. Bare. And altogether too vulnerable.

"I…" she started.

But before she could finish, the frosted glass window at the counter slid open with a horrible screech.

Tessa whipped her head in the direction of the sound.

The woman behind the counter narrowed her gaze. "Can I help you?"

"Yes, I need to speak to the company secretary. Or possibly Madame Daria, if she's available." Tessa swallowed. This was more difficult than she'd thought it would be. "I need to withdraw from the auditions."

The woman looked her up and down and then shrugged. "I'm the company secretary, and I'm afraid you're too late."

Tessa frowned. "Too late?"

"What's your name, dear?"

"Tessa Wilde."

The older woman winked. "You should probably go check the list."

Tessa's heart nearly stopped.

"The casting list is up? Already?" Ivanov had already chosen his dancers? After just two days?

Impossible. Auditions were scheduled to go through this evening.

"It went up about ten minutes ago." The secretary shot her an encouraging smile. "Good luck."

Right.

Tessa turned, not really expecting to see the piano

man still standing there. But all the same, she felt a bittersweet tug of disappointment when she realized he'd gone.

It doesn't matter. He doesn't matter. At the moment, only one thing did. The casting list.

She strode toward the practice studio, where the casting sheet was most likely tacked to the door so it couldn't be missed. Other dancers rushed past her, eager to check for their names. Word had obviously spread. The air hummed with anticipation. Tessa could feel it as surely as she could feel the lingering butterflies in her stomach from her intriguing encounter with the piano player.

Her footsteps danced a fine line between a walk and a run. Up ahead, she could see Violet's wide grin as she hugged one of the girls who'd shared the barre with them the day before in class. Good. They'd both been chosen, possibly even placed in Cast A.

Every ballet had two different casts that performed on alternating nights. Cast A was the more prestigious grouping, the crème de la crème. They performed opening night, when all the critics typically showed up. Cast A always closed the show, as well. Cast B, in turn, performed matinees and weekday nights.

As she reached the cluster of dancers crowded around the door to the practice studio, the floor began to vibrate. Dancers jumped up and down, their excitement so real that it was a tangible, physical force, humming beneath Tessa's feet. There was a lot of noise, too—so many voices that Tessa couldn't have made sense of them even if they hadn't sounded so muffled and strange.

A ribbon of dread snaked through her as she stood on the fringe of the crowd. She wanted to look, but at the same time, she didn't. If her name wasn't printed on the sheet of paper tacked to the door, it was over. Everything. Her dancing. Her life. As long as she didn't know—as long as there was still a glimmer of hope—nothing changed. She was still a ballerina.

What are you thinking? You came here to quit, remember?

In front of her, Violet turned around to head out of the crush of bodies and make room for the ones who hadn't yet pored over the list. Tessa had never seen her friend look so happy, so full of joy. *Cast A. Definitely.* Then Violet made eye contact with Tessa, and her smile faded. Just the tiniest bit.

So the news was bad.

"It's okay," Tessa said, as her limbs went wooden. She'd expected failure to feel different, somehow. She'd expected soul-crushing disappointment and tears. Definitely tears.

But the tears didn't come. Neither did the sadness. She felt nothing, actually. Just a strange state of numbness, as if her body refused to acknowledge the awful reality of the situation. This one, final loss was more than she could accept. She wished she'd had the chance to quit. At least then she would have never known she hadn't been good enough.

"I'm sorry," Violet said, gathering Tessa in her arms and holding on tight.

Tessa couldn't even bring herself to hug Violet back. She just stood there awkwardly, until her friend finally let her go. She wasn't sure what perverse drive compelled her to look at the list when she knew she wouldn't find her name on it. Closure, perhaps? Or maybe she just needed to see its absence for herself. Then maybe the awful truth would sink in.

She pushed her way to the front of the crowd and scanned the list of corps dancers for Cast A. As expected, Violet's name was right there. Second from the bottom, but placement didn't matter. She was in. Tessa, of course, was not. Her name was nowhere to be found. Her gaze flitted to the Cast B corps list. It wasn't there either. So this was real. She was finished.

She stood for a second, until she imagined she could feel her heart breaking in two. But as she turned to go, her gaze snagged on a familiar arrangement of letters.

Her name.

She whipped her head back around and scanned the list again. She still didn't see it. Great. Now she wasn't just hearing things, she was hallucinating. Just in case, she let her gaze drift upward, past the list of corps dancers. She read the names of the dancers who'd been selected for solo parts, and then finally stopped reading when she reached the very top of the page.

There it was.

Tessa Wilde.

It had to be some kind of mistake. What was her name doing opposite the lead role? In Cast A? It just wasn't possible.

Was it?

Violet certainly hadn't seen it. Then again, she'd been looking at the list of corps dancers, not the principals.

The lead role—the diamond tutu—it was all too much to hope for. It wasn't real. Just like the sound. Just like the music. None of this was real.

Then, through the slender window on the door, she caught a glimpse of the man sitting at the piano. His back was to her as he pounded on the Steinway, his nimble hands flying over the keys, the same elegant hands he'd used to speak to her only moments ago.

Congratulations.

He'd known.

Somehow it made sense that he had. She wasn't sure why or how. But it did.

Chapter Five

"I hate to say I told you so." Against all odds, Julian found himself smiling as he sat across from Chance at the coffee shop around the corner from the dance studio. As close as he ever came to smiling, anyway.

"But you're going to." Chance rolled his eyes as he drained his espresso. He seemed antsy. In a hurry to run off and bed one of his coworkers, most likely. "Go ahead. Say it."

"Okay." Julian shrugged. "I told you she was good, and I was right."

He grinned into his cup of coffee. He preferred it black. Bitter. Like his mood. Although at the moment his mood wasn't half-bad. A rarity.

What had gotten into him, anyway? He was out for coffee. He was chatting with a friend. Anyone watching would have thought he lived a normal life, full of outings and social engagements. The life of the party. He probably even looked like the old Julian right about now.

Except for the scars.

"You certainly did. It seems your little Tessa has turned you into a balletomane," Chance said.

"She's not mine. And it doesn't take an expert to see that she's good. Admit it." *Your* little Tessa. He wished Chance would stop using that particular adjective. Although, if it kept Chance from sleeping with her, he supposed he could live with it.

Since when do you care whom she sleeps with?

He didn't. Of course he didn't. He just thought she deserved better than Chance. He was a friend, yes. But also a player. Not that he needed to lose any sleep over Tessa's love life, he reminded himself.

She'd been crossing his mind more than he cared to admit. If he was really being honest, she could possibly be the reason for the sudden uptick in his mood. Which was just absurd.

So Tessa had been given a role. A *lead* role. But so what? They'd hardly even spoken to each other. It had nothing to do with him.

You're happy for her. You care.

Right. Not likely. His change in mood was more probably attributed to the fact that he could taunt Chance unmercifully because he'd been right about Tessa all along. She was a gorgeous dancer. Special. Chance had to have been blind not to notice.

Even if Julian did care—just a little—the feeling was obviously not mutual. Tessa had looked at him as though he'd sprouted a second head when he'd signed at her earlier.

Congratulations.

He probably hadn't even gotten it right. So much for YouTube tutorials. He forced his lips into a straight line and tried not to think about the fact that his first instinct upon seeing her name at the top of the casting sheet had been to Google "how to congratulate someone in sign language."

What was he doing?

"Yeah, well, you were right. She's good." Chance shrugged. "Big deal."

A nonsensical spike of irritation hit Julian square in the chest, which only irritated him further. "That's a little harsh, don't you think? You've been cast as her partner, remember?"

"Exactly." Chance gave his empty demitasse cup a shove toward the edge of the table. He drummed his fingers on the tabletop. "Pardon me if I'm less than thrilled at being cast in the lead alongside a dancer who wasn't even part of the company until this week. A deaf dancer at that."

Julian's grip on his coffee mug tightened. "Don't be such an ass. You're still the star of the show."

"For now," Chance said.

Julian stared blankly at him. "What more do you want?"

Chance's gaze narrowed. "You don't get it, do you?"

Apparently not. "Enlighten me."

"If she screws this up, we're done. Which means *I'm* done. We rehearse as partners. If she can't cut it—and I sincerely doubt she can—they'll move the Cast B lead couple up to Cast A, and the understudies would become Cast B."

Julian sighed and then reminded himself that none of this had anything to do with him. He played the piano in the corner. He was invisible, and that's just the way he wanted it. "I guess I thought once the casts were chosen, they were set in stone."

"Every part, every step of choreography—hell, even every costume—is subject to change up until the moment you're onstage. Nothing is ever set in stone in ballet."

Or life.

Julian knew as much. All too well. Wasn't there a Grammy Award sitting on the mantel in the apartment he could barely afford? The night he'd brought that shiny gold statue home should have been the beginning of his song. Instead, it had turned out to be the *outro*.

He swallowed. The coffee had left a bad taste in his mouth. Now he remembered why he never did this sort of thing anymore. "Tessa's got a shot, though. Maybe you can help her."

"Me? I'm a dancer, not a social worker." Chance let out a bitter laugh.

Every so often, when Julian was with Chance, he caught a glimpse of the lanky kid who'd grown up across the street from him in Brooklyn. Now was not one of those moments. Chance had long shaken off any of his lingering awkwardness. He was a star, from the tips of his toes to the top of his arrogant head. Sometimes Julian wondered how their friendship had survived.

But deep down, he knew it was because he and

Chance were the same. There was nothing gallant about Julian. There never had been. Not even before. It had taken a single-minded focus to come as far as he had. He'd had time for nothing but himself. There'd been women, but they hadn't meant anything. Julian's life had been all about Julian. And his music, of course.

But the music had just been an extension. It had been a part of him as much as his legs, his arms, his hands.

His face.

He cleared his throat. He didn't give a damn about the scars. Not really. It was what they represented—the loss of the music—that made him hate looking in the mirror.

He put down his coffee cup. "Believe me, I know you're no social worker. It's just a suggestion. You're her partner after all. If she doesn't dance, you don't dance. You said so yourself."

"So you're saying I should spend every night at the studio, just like Tessa?"

"No. That's not what I said at all. There are other ways, you know." He focused intently on the wood grain of the table between them. "Probably, anyway."

Chance narrowed his gaze. "As in?"

Julian feigned nonchalance as best he could. "Non-auditory cues. Something visual or sensory for her to rely on for timing with your partnering."

Chance stared at him for a long, silent moment. When he finally spoke, there was an unmistakable hint of amusement in his tone. "Since when have you become an expert on hearing impairment?"

Damn Google. Julian had the sudden urge to pitch

his cell phone into the nearest black hole. "Look, surely there are things you can do to make it easier on her. I'm guessing there are, anyway."

"You're just guessing. Got it." Chance winked. "*Nonauditory cues* is just a phrase that came to you off the top of your head."

Julian's temples throbbed. "Can we change the subject?"

"Gladly. Let's get out of here. I've got a date tonight." Of course he did.

Chance rose from his chair and tossed a few dollar bills on the table—enough to cover both their coffees. Julian didn't bother reaching for his wallet. It would have been a waste of time. Since the night of the accident, he'd become Chance's project. The job, the coffees, the unexpected visits…guilt offerings. If it had been anyone else, Julian wouldn't have put up with it. He had his pride after all.

Outside the coffeehouse, a street performer had set up business on the corner of 66th and Amsterdam. A percussionist. He'd arranged his drumsticks in a neat row on the sidewalk, on top of a red towel. Julian's footsteps slowed as he passed, and his gaze narrowed. The drumsticks were Vaters. The real deal. The guy sounded good, too, even though he was using those nice sticks on a pair of upturned plastic buckets, rather than actual drums. *Ratatatatatatatat*.

Julian's hand thumped against the side of his thigh in time with the beat as he and Chance crossed the street and headed uptown. Even after the *thump thump thump* of the drummer's sticks faded and blended with the sounds of the city—sirens, horns, the whoosh of traffic—the rhythm hummed in Julian's fingertips.

There'd been a time when he'd heard music everywhere. He hadn't even tried. He'd step out of his apartment door and lose himself in the staccato of street noises. Songs seemed to write themselves. He'd been able to find a pattern even in the most random collection of noises. All around him, the city had moved and breathed, spinning free-form jazz improvisations in his head. He'd been a songwriter, and New York had been his song.

After the accident, after he'd stopped playing, he'd also stopped listening. It hadn't been a conscious decision. Somehow, the music had just slipped away. He didn't tap his toes anymore to jackhammer noises on street corners. He didn't hear low bass moans in the breaths of idle bus engines. Somehow, in the loudest city in the world, Julian's soul had gone silent.

He was beginning to hear it again, though.

He didn't know how. Or why. Maybe playing the piano had unlocked something inside him. Maybe the explanation wasn't so simple.

Maybe, as much as he didn't want to admit it, his reawakening was in some way related to Tessa. Something shifted inside him when he watched her dance. He lost himself in her fluid grace, much like the way he used to lose himself in his music.

He felt almost whole again, which was borderline nuts. His behavior didn't make any sense. What was he doing Googling ASL and nonauditory cues? If Tessa found out about it, she'd probably think he was some sort of stalker.

Whatever the reason, he was once again beginning to find the rhythm in everyday life.

He'd strummed a five-part melody against his leg for two blocks, distracted by the faint stirring of a song that seemed to be fighting its way to the forefront of his consciousness, before he realized Chance was leading him in the exact opposite direction from the 66th Street station.

Julian stopped. Chance kept on walking.

"Hey, man," he called after him. "Where are you going?"

"Not much farther." Chance walked a few more feet and then turned around. "Okay. Here."

Julian approached him slowly. What the hell was going on?

Chance crossed his arms and waited in front of the Bennington Hotel, one of the most famous historic hotels in Manhattan. The Bennington was an icon of the Roaring Twenties, as well as the home of Guy Lombardo and his orchestra and the birthplace of the New York tradition of playing "Auld Lang Syne" on New Year's Eve. Julian knew a lot about the Bennington. What he didn't know was why he was standing beneath its glittering marquee while the midtown traffic moved behind him in a blur of yellow taxis and sleek black town cars.

Dread settled in the pit of his stomach. He wasn't sure why, but he had a bad feeling about this. Very bad.

"I'm not dressed for drinks here, if that's what you

have in mind." Julian cast a pointed glance at a man dressed in a sleek tuxedo, who was entering the building through its shiny revolving door, and then narrowed his gaze at Chance. "Neither are you, for that matter."

Chance shook his head. "Not drinks. I just want to show you something. Let's go inside. It'll take five minutes, tops. Then you can go home and get back to your busy schedule of ignoring the rest of the world."

Chance shoved his hands into the pockets of his hoodie and disappeared through the revolving door. Julian had no choice but to follow.

It had been a while since he'd set foot inside the Bennington. Years. But the sight of the grand lobby, with its shimmering chandelier, expansive floor and elegant columns, took him right back. Not just to *his* past, but to *the* past—the era he loved most. The Jazz Age.

A ribbon of nostalgia wound its way through him, and somewhere in the back of his head, he heard a Count Basie song. Then he saw the sign tucked into the far corner of the lobby, and his suspicions were confirmed.

Mystery solved.

"The Circle Club?" He glared at Chance. "You've dragged me to a jazz club?"

Chance glared right back at him. "No. I've dragged you to a soon-to-be jazz club. It's not open yet."

"Then there's nothing to see or hear. Let's go." He turned on his heel and stalked back toward the revolving doors. How the hell had he let Chance lead him down here to begin with?

Chance caught up with him when he reached the spot

beneath the huge hanging clock in front of the registration desk. Sooner than he would have liked. He would have actually preferred not to see Chance's face again for the foreseeable future. Julian wasn't an idiot. He knew where this was going.

"Come on, man. Hear me out," Chance said. "The club doesn't open for another month, and they're looking for performers."

And there it was.

Julian spun around. "I don't play the trumpet anymore. You know that," he said through gritted teeth.

"You play the piano," Chance said calmly. Too calmly, actually. He'd obviously given the matter some thought and was prepared for whatever arguments Julian threw at him.

"I play the piano for a *ballet company.* Anyone with half a brain could do it. In case you haven't noticed, I'm not exactly Thelonious Monk."

Chance shrugged. "But you could be."

"Have you lost your mind?" Clearly he had, or they wouldn't be having this conversation. Thelonious Monk was a legend. Julian most assuredly was not.

Not anymore, anyway.

"You're a songwriter. You've been a songwriter since the middle school talent show." Sometimes Julian really hated that Chance had known him for so long. "You don't need a trumpet to write songs."

Technically, that might be true. But not for Julian. He couldn't just start over. Not now. Even if he could stand the humiliation, he doubted he still had what it took to climb back up again from the bottom. Making it in the music world took more than talent. It took drive and determination. A hunger for success.

He'd been hungry once. He wasn't anymore. Now he was just tired. So damned tired.

Whatever Chance expected from him was too much. Playing the piano was one thing. Writing music—*performing*, for crying out loud—those were different things entirely. Things that belonged in the past. In a life that was no longer his.

"Forget it. Not happening," he said and realized his hand had stopped tapping against his leg. His arms now hung loosely at his sides. The Count Basie tune in his head had gone quiet.

Chance sighed. "Just tell me you'll think about it."

"There's nothing to think about." He was practically yelling now. People in the hotel's opulent lobby were beginning to stare. Julian didn't care. He just needed Chance to stop. For once and for all. "Look, I took the job. I'm back on my feet. You can quit now. You're officially off the hook."

"Off the hook?" Chance's tone had a sudden bite to it. "You think this is about the accident?"

"Isn't it? Isn't that what *everything* has been about for the past two years? The visits, the job and now this?" He waved an arm toward the sign for the future The Circle Club. The letters were gold leaf on black, straight out of *The Great Gatsby*.

"Actually, no. This is about friendship." Chance took a step closer, directly into Julian's personal space. Were they going to actually fight about this? Brawl in the

Bennington like F. Scott Fitzgerald would have done back in the day?

Maybe.

Doubtful, though. As satisfying as it might be to take a swing at Chance's meddling face, Julian would feel like a grade-A ass later on if he actually went through with it.

He sighed. "You can stop feeling guilty, Chance. It wasn't your fault. You were the one behind the wheel, but it could have just as easily been me. We're even. You don't owe me a thing."

Tension rolled off Chance in waves. Julian had underestimated how much he was invested in this whole jazz club idea. Of course, that didn't change anything. Julian still wanted nothing to do with it. "For the record, I never thought I owed you. I just hate seeing you like this."

"Then stop looking." Julian's clenched his fists at his sides.

He needed to get out of there. Away from Chance, and away from his nonsensical expectations. He'd put up with his friend's gentle prodding since the day he'd come home from the hospital. As much as he hated it, he'd managed to ignore it. He figured whatever weird sort of survivor's guilt Chance felt would eventually wear off. After all, Julian wasn't dead.

But it wasn't wearing off. If anything, it was getting worse. Now he wanted Julian to write songs again? To get up and perform in front of an audience? Not just a bunch of dancers who thought of him as a prop, but a roomful of people who'd paid a cover charge to see him?

Hell, no.

Next he'd expect Julian to do something about his attraction to Tessa. Yeah, that wasn't happening either. He wasn't about to give Chance that kind of satisfaction.

Is that the only thing holding you back?

No. Julian had his reasons, though. Good ones. The number one reason happened to be the fact that relationships led to pressure and expectations, and he was experiencing enough of those at the moment. The number two reason was as plain as the scar on his face.

There were scars, obviously. Chance had been removed from the vehicle before the fire started. Julian hadn't been so lucky. He'd suffered third-degree burns on his left side, from his torso to his thigh, before the rescue team had dragged him out.

"I'm leaving," he said.

He turned around but stopped cold before he could step out from beneath the hanging clock's shadow. There she was.

Tessa.

In the flesh, as if his thoughts had somehow summoned her.

She was walking through the gilded revolving door, wearing a buttercup-yellow dress and looking like she'd stepped right out of a dream. She had a dog leash in her hand, and the tiny dog Julian had seen her with on the subway was trotting merrily at the end of it.

Julian's gaze traveled from the fluffy little dog to the graceful turn of Tessa's wrist as she held the leash to the exquisite planes of her heart-shaped face—emerald eyes, delicate cheekbones, full, kissable lips.

He went hard.

God, she was beautiful. He knew that already, obviously. But seeing her surrounded by so much art deco elegance did something to him. It made him ache. In a good way, like Nina Simone sang about in "Feeling Good."

She caught his gaze and smiled. Julian glowered at her.

What was going on? Was this some kind of romantic ambush? Had Chance invited her to meet them here? If so, he'd taken things too far. *Way* too far.

But as Tessa's smile faded, a guy in an impeccably cut suit swooped to her side and kissed her on the cheek. Tessa tore her gaze away from Julian, wrapped her willowy arms around the stranger and gave him a hug. Julian's teeth clenched involuntarily.

She was on a date. Marvelous.

"What's wrong?" Chance sidled up next to Julian and followed his gaze. "Is that Tessa? It is. Damn, she looks fantastic."

As if Julian hadn't noticed.

"Let's go," he said, but for some idiotic reason, his feet refused to move.

Chance shot him a bemused grin. "Not in such a hurry to go now, are you, friend?"

Tessa glanced over Zander's shoulder as he wrapped her in his arms, searching for another glimpse of the utterly handsome man who'd been staring at her when she walked into the lobby. The utterly handsome, utterly *familiar-looking* man.

It was him. The piano player. She'd recognize that scowl anywhere.

Sure enough, when Zander released her and took a step back, she got a clear look. Same brooding blue eyes. Same ridiculously masculine jawline.

Same butterflies in her stomach.

"Tessa." Zander gave her arm a little squeeze.

She dragged her attention back to her brother. "Sorry. I was distracted." *By the musical Prince Charming standing right over there.*

Prince Charming? Hardly. Prince of Darkness was more like it. Why was he glaring at her like that? The last time they'd seen each other, they'd had a pleasant exchange. Sort of, anyway. And what was he doing at the Bennington? Her brother had been CEO of the hotel for three years running, and she'd never seen him here before. Chance Gabel either.

"Congratulations!" Zander signed the word, but spoke at the same time. Tessa tried, and failed, to force the sound of his voice into the proper syllables. There were too many extraneous sounds in the hotel lobby— street noises drifting in through the revolving door, telephones ringing, snippets of conversations from the elegantly attired people milling about, the ding of the elevator. Everything blended together into one constant, droning hum.

She forced a smile and nodded. "Thank you. And thanks so much for tonight."

Truthfully, she'd rather be at home swimming in silence and resting for her first day of rehearsal as a company dancer tomorrow. But her family would never have accepted that she wouldn't want to celebrate. Unless she told them the truth, which was definitely out of the question.

"We're all thrilled for you, Tessa. I knew you could do it, you know." Zander wrapped an arm around her shoulders and then seemed to notice her preoccupation with the piano player's unwavering gaze.

Tessa swallowed. She felt like she was in some kind of sexy staring contest. And the flutter in her belly seemed like a guarantee she'd never win.

She very purposefully looked away.

Zander's lips moved. "Do you know him?"

"Yes," she said while, at the same time, shaking her head. "I mean no."

Zander lifted a brow. "Which is it? Yes or no?"

"No." Because she didn't know him. Not really. Besides, he had a definite air about him that conveyed he didn't wish to be known. By anyone.

Most of the time, anyway.

There'd been a few solicitous moments—times when he'd trained his gaze on her, and she'd glimpsed an undeniable tenderness in his soulful blue eyes. Moments that had left her inexplicably breathless.

She tried to swallow, but her mouth went dry.

Then to her great embarrassment, Mr. B decided to make a liar out of her by sprinting toward the piano player with such enthusiasm that his leash flew out of her hand.

Oh, my God. "Mr. B! Come back here."

Tessa watched in horror as her dog launched himself at the enigmatic man, pawing frantically at his shins.

She called Mr. B's name a few more times, but he didn't bother batting a doggy eyelid in her direction. Mr. B was usually so well behaved. His fascination with Julian was so strange. And so very, very mortifying.

Zander touched her arm again, dragging her attention away from the train wreck in progress. He shot her a sardonic grin. "You might not know him, but your dog certainly does."

With a sigh, Tessa darted off in pursuit of Mr. B. Zander followed. Of course he did. She couldn't blame him, she supposed.

It had been a while since she'd been interested in anyone romantically. Not since before her accident. If she'd been born deaf, maybe the fact that she couldn't hear wouldn't have felt so isolating. There was a tangle of silence between her and the outside world that most men weren't interested in unraveling. The fact that Tessa had been too busy adjusting to her new reality to unravel it herself only compounded the problem.

Zander was jumping to the wrong conclusion, obviously. Butterflies notwithstanding, there was nothing romantic going on between her and the piano player. Life had decided to throw her into a tailspin at the most important time in her dance career. She had enough on her plate.

Plus he worked with the ballet company. She obviously couldn't date him. Or heaven forbid, sleep with him. She didn't even know his name.

Right. Then why are you picturing it in your head right now?

She blinked. Hard. But somehow she couldn't quite

rid herself of the image of the two of them in one of the Bennington's luxurious beds.

What was wrong with her?

"I'm sorry." She bent to snatch Mr. B in her arms and then stood, finding herself eye to eye with the brooding man in question. "So, so sorry."

His gaze flitted to Zander. Just for a second. When he redirected his attention back to Tessa, his expression remained unchanged. Guarded. But then he lifted his hand and gave her a little wave.

Hi.

The butterflies multiplied a thousandfold. Tessa was surprised she didn't float right off the ground. "Hi."

Zander looked back and forth between them. So did Chance. Tessa suddenly felt like she was onstage, part of a duet that she hadn't prepared for. Hadn't rehearsed.

She cleared her throat.

Zander stuck out his hand. "Hello. Since my sister apparently isn't going to introduce us, I'm Zander Wilde."

"Julian Shine." He shook her brother's hand.

Tessa stared intently at his lips, desperate to get his name right. *Julian Shine.* It sounded vaguely familiar. Maybe she'd seen it somewhere on the ballet company's website, when she'd registered for her audition.

She wasn't sure. Likewise, she wasn't sure if Julian seemed relieved when Zander announced that he was her brother, or if she was reading too much into the loosening of his posture. She tried not to think about it as Chance and Zander exchanged pleasantries and Mr. B squirmed in her arms.

Introductions complete, Zander immediately turned

his attention back to Julian. "Julian Shine, as in *the* Julian Shine?"

The grimace on Julian's face was unmistakable.

Chance nodded and answered for him. "The one and only."

"It's an honor to meet you. Truly." Zander motioned toward the far corner of the lobby. "Fortuitous, too. We're opening a jazz bar in a few weeks."

"Julian and I were just discussing that very thing," Chance said.

Julian stared daggers at him. Chance didn't so much as flinch.

"I'd love to sit down and discuss it with you sometime." Zander grinned.

What on earth was her brother doing?

Had he not noticed the look of extreme disinterest on Julian's face? His glower could probably be seen from space.

"Um, I don't think…" Tessa interrupted.

Zander pressed on. "We have a monthly Big Band Night in the ballroom. The next one is two weeks from Sunday. If you come by, I can comp you dinner and a room."

Julian shook his head. "I appreciate the offer, but I don't play anymore."

Tessa frowned. "Yes, you do."

"I play the piano," Julian conceded. "But it's not the same."

Not the same? What was she missing? And why had her brother asked him if he was *the* Julian Shine?

"That's fine. You don't need to play." Zander reached

into his pocket for a business card and offered it to Julian. "Just come enjoy the evening."

"Thank you. I'll check my schedule." Julian took the card. Judging from his expression, he was more likely to volunteer for a root canal than take her brother up on his offer.

He gave Mr. B a pat on the head, waved goodbye to Tessa and disappeared before Zander could entreat him further.

"He'll be there. I'll see to it," Chance said and then fell in step behind his friend.

Zander's gaze followed them out of the hotel's spinning door. As did Mr. B's. Clearly, Tessa wasn't the only one charmed by the perpetually cranky Julian Shine.

As the two men exited, Tessa's other family members spun their way inside the building. Her mother. Her cousin. Even her elusive sister.

Before they got within earshot, Tessa gave Zander's shoulder a firm jab. "What was *that*?"

Zander frowned at her and adjusted one of his cuff links. "I beg your pardon?"

"With Julian… Asking him about the jazz club and then inviting him to Big Band Night?" She always turned up for that. Her family made sure she did. "Are you trying to set us up?"

"What? No. Absolutely not." Zander shook his head for added emphasis. "He's a player. Or at least, he used to be before his accident."

Tessa's heart began to beat hard in her chest. "How do you know all of this? And what accident?"

She tightened her hold on Mr. B as the haunting

memory of an ambulance siren wailed in her consciousness. It had been the last sound she'd ever heard.

Until Julian's music yesterday.

"Julian Shine is one of the best jazz musicians of all time. A trumpet player. He's right up there with Miles Davis and Wynton Marsalis. He was, anyway. He was in a bad car accident a while back. Since then, he's pretty much been a recluse." Zander gave her a grim smile. "It's a shame, really. The guy's a legend."

A legend who'd apparently suffered a career-ending accident, just as Tessa had. Finally, an explanation for the permanent frown. Everything was suddenly crystal clear...

Everything except the way Tessa felt when that frown was aimed in her direction. Alive. Special. And seen.

Seen like never before.

Chapter Six

As it turned out, Tessa had a lot more to worry about on her first day of rehearsal than her hearing. Or her undeniable fascination with Julian Shine.

Ivanov's choreography for the *pas de deux*, her duet with Chance, included a lift. She'd expected this, of course. Lifts were almost always a major part of any *pas de deux*. But typically they were more toward the middle, or even the end, of the duet, so she thought she'd have a day or two to get acclimated to her new role, before being hoisted into the air.

She'd been wrong. Dreadfully wrong. Ivanov's *pas de deux* started with a lift. Not just any lift either. The opening move was an angel lift—the most dangerous partnering move of all.

It also happened to be the exact lift that Tessa and

her partner had been doing when she'd fallen and hit her head.

Alexei Ivanov had no way of knowing this, of course. And Tessa had no intention of telling him. She wasn't even sure he knew about her deafness. Most of the dancers did, since so many of them had trained at the Wilde School of Dance in their preprofessional lives. Madame Daria might have known, but Tessa wasn't certain. The ballet mistress was a rigid taskmistress and wouldn't have treated Tessa any differently had she known. Which was a good thing, as far as Tessa was concerned.

But Alexei Ivanov was new to New York, and Tessa was quite certain he'd never heard of her before this week.

She debated whether or not she should tell him. Her mother insisted that Tessa should. At Tessa's celebratory dinner at the Bennington, Emily Wilde had mentioned it more than once. Probably more than two or three times. Tessa wasn't sure. Her thoughts kept drifting back to Julian when she should have been reading lips. It didn't matter, though. She'd already decided not to say anything to the choreographer about her hearing loss or the accident.

She didn't want to be seen as weak, lest he reconsider casting her in the lead. Also, the timing couldn't have been worse. Tessa could hear out of her right ear now…sort of. Looking Ivanov in the eye and telling him she was deaf would feel like lying. And she certainly couldn't admit she was in the middle of some kind of medical crisis. He'd dismiss her on the spot.

The way she saw it, she had no choice but to show

up and perform well enough to prove herself worthy of being chosen to dance a principal role in a major New York ballet company. All she'd wanted all along was to be treated like any other ballerina, and now was her chance.

The trouble began when Chance put his hands on her waist. Until then, on the rare occasions when Tessa allowed herself to remember her fall, she'd seen it as a slide show flickering in her consciousness. An old-time silent movie with muted Kodachrome colors and slow-motion shadows.

Her memory was what she'd always imagined an out-of-body experience must feel like, but even that wasn't quite right. She felt removed from what had happened. Detached. Like it hadn't actually happened to her, but to another girl entirely. Some young ballet hopeful who Tessa had never met—a girl with beautifully arched feet, a straight, supple back and stars in her eyes.

That girl bore such little resemblance to the person Tessa saw in the mirrored walls of the ballet studio, she felt like a disinterested spectator. It was as if she'd never even been in the studio that day, never set foot on that moon-gray Marley floor, never felt the rush of wind through her hair as she'd been lifted in the air. But rather like she'd been outside on the snowy Manhattan sidewalk, with her face pressed to the window, breath fogging the glass as she watched in horror while the boy stumbled and the pretty ballerina in his arms went tumbling to the ground.

When Chance touched her, when the warmth of his hands pressed against her leotard, it all came rushing back.

She remembered details that had somehow become lost over the years—the way Owen's hands shook during their opening promenade, the clean soap smell of his white T-shirt. She remembered everything, from the tremulous smile on his lips when she'd launched herself into his hands to the final horrifying sound after her free fall—the nauseating crack of her skull banging against the studio floor.

Tessa wanted to press her hands against her ears and block it out. She probably would have, if the entire cast hadn't been there watching. Madame Daria. Violet. All the other ballerinas who'd been passed over for the lead, standing with their arms crossed, feigning nonchalance as they waited for her to screw up, to make some fatal mistake.

And Julian, sitting at the piano.

He was watching her with an intensity that made heat gather and pool in her center. What was it about that man? She shouldn't be attracted to him. She absolutely shouldn't. Most days, he was borderline rude. His car wreck had clearly left him bitter.

But Tessa could understand that, probably more than most other people could. And her dog liked him. A lot, which was a surprise. Mr. B had always had such discriminating taste. His fondness for Julian had nothing to do with the butterfly wings that beat against the inside of her rib cage every time he looked at her, though.

Julian had signed for her. He'd spoken to her with his hands. And when he did, it had felt almost as if he'd taken a step inside her world of silence.

No man had ever done that for her before. Not even the man who at one time had wanted to marry her.

He wasn't very good at it. He was quite terrible actually, but somehow that made his efforts all the more endearing. She liked it when he used those musical hands of his to talk to her. He had lovely hands. She wondered what it might feel like to be touched by those hands, those skillful, poetic fingers. Treasured, probably. Like a rare instrument. A Stradivarius.

She gave him a nervous smile from the center of the practice-room floor. He smiled back.

God, what was wrong with her? Could there possibly be a worse time to flirt? *Focus.*

Chance gave her waist a squeeze, a signal for her to look at him. Which she should have been doing in the first place.

"Ready?" he mouthed.

No. Absolutely not. "Yes." She nodded firmly.

He backed away a few feet.

Tessa took a calming breath, closed her rib cage and found her center, just as Julian struck his first chord on the piano. The music flowed through her with liquid confidence, and she lifted into an arabesque. The moment Chance's hands found her waist, she arched her back and transferred all her weight into his grasp. He pushed her up, up, up in the air, and her arms floated overhead like angel wings.

For a split second, Tessa felt as though she were flying. Free, like an airy, ethereal bird. Like starlight. For the first time in as long as she could remember, she felt whole. Her earlier apprehension seemed silly. Then she looked down, searching for Julian.

Huge mistake.

The floor was so far away. Impossibly far. And so solid. Her stomach began to churn, and her mouth went bone-dry.

She squeezed her eyes closed. Her gaze should have been fixed on a focal point. She should have been spotting, just as if she'd been in a turn.

She didn't know why she'd sought Julian out. Again. She knew better, but she'd allowed herself to get lost in the music, the moment. There was also a part of her that wanted to see his face as he watched her the way she used to be. For reasons she didn't quite understand, she had a strange yearning for him to see her that way. Bold. Unbroken. Whole.

The very second she looked down, she felt her balance slip. Ever so slightly. Her center of gravity tipped just a fraction too far forward, and rather than waiting for Chance to make the proper adjustments in his grip and stance—as she *should* have done—she dropped her arms. Her sudden change in position killed the lift. She grabbed Chance's shoulders and clawed at the cotton fabric of his white T-shirt, gathering it in her fists like a frightened child clutches a blanket.

Then everything went silent, just as it had the last time, right after she'd hit her head. The music simply stopped, as if she'd been imagining it all along, just as she feared.

She opened her eyes and saw Julian, his face pale,

sitting at the piano. He'd stopped playing and was instead staring at her and Chance, which explained the sudden silence.

She looked down at the floor spinning beneath her and thought she might be sick. Chance stumbled, and she screamed, convinced it was happening all over again.

She was going to fall.

Right there, in front of everyone.

Julian could feel the piano keys beneath his fingertips, but he couldn't seem to make his hands move. His breath caught in his throat, and his heart stopped beating, as surely as it had the night of his car accident.

She's falling.

Tessa was all out of balance. She was going to smash right into the ground, and there was nothing he could do about it.

Everything had gone eerily quiet. Still. The world around him was moving in slow motion. Then, just as quickly as it began, the silence came to an abrupt end.

People starting shouting, all at the same time. Chance tried to tell Tessa to lean further forward. She'd shied away from the ground and shifted her center of gravity, pulling him off balance. Julian could see it. Everyone could.

Madame Daria clapped her hands and yelled, "Tessa, lift from your core. Lift!"

The Russian got out of his chair and screamed corrections. "Hold it. Save the lift. Find your balance. Hold!"

Tessa couldn't hear any of it, obviously. Even if she could, it was too late. There was no saving the lift.

Tessa scrambled down Chance's body like a frightened animal inching its way down a tree. Chance swayed a little on his feet. His hands tightened around her waist, digging into her flesh until he managed to set her down on the ground. Gently. Deliberately. As if to prove a point.

She was safe.

Chance was an experienced partner. Julian knew that as well as anyone. Tessa had probably been safe all along. But it hadn't looked that way to Julian, and it clearly hadn't felt that way to Tessa, as she'd been suspended so far up in the air.

Julian stared down at his hands. They were balled into tight fists in his lap now. In his panic, he'd given up even the pretense of trying to play the piano. Chance's words from the other day kept spinning round and round in his head.

She had an accident a year or so ago. A ballet accident. Her partner dropped her during a lift, and she hit her head.

She must have been terrified just now.

The Russian was still screaming at the top of his lungs, and Julian wanted nothing more than to jump up and wring his pompous neck. Chance cut Julian a sharp glance. It was a clear warning. *Stay out of it.*

Tessa stared down at her pink pointe shoes and maintained her death grip on Chance's T-shirt, while Julian struggled to remain seated.

It's not your business.

It had nothing to do with him. He and Tessa had only exchanged a handful of words. But Julian couldn't shake the feeling that there was something there. Some kind of tenuous connection.

He wanted her.

Obviously.

He'd wanted her since the moment he set eyes on her. Even before he'd seen her dance, he'd been drawn to her fragile strength. Her kindness. She was everything that he wasn't. In a way, they were flip sides of the same coin. Perhaps that's why she stirred something in him. She touched him somewhere deep inside…a part of him that he'd thought he'd lost.

He had no intention of acting on the attraction. None whatsoever, even though seeing her at the Bennington with another man had made him realize just how much he despised the thought of her with anyone else. Relief had flowed through him like warm honey when Zander had introduced himself as Tessa's brother. Pure, unadulterated relief.

All the same, he wasn't fit for a relationship. He never had been, and he *certainly* wasn't now. Even Chance was almost ready to give up on him since he'd refused to even discuss Zander's invitation from the night before. Julian was almost glad the attraction he felt for Tessa didn't appear to be reciprocated.

And yet, in the moments before fear set in, and she'd started to fall out of the lift, Julian could have sworn she'd intentionally sought him out. Her gaze locked with his, and the joy he'd seen in the depths of her emerald eyes had taken his breath away. It had been the most beautiful damn thing he'd ever seen.

But what had it meant?

"What the hell was that? That lift could have easily been saved. I told you what to do—close your ribs, tighten your core, find your focal point. You didn't even try. Why didn't you listen?" Ivanov threw his arms in the air and stalked toward Tessa.

She didn't answer him. Nor did she turn around, probably because she couldn't hear the criticism coming from the Russian's mouth.

Julian was glad. Tessa didn't need to hear it. She was already shaken up enough as it was. But Ivanov either didn't notice or he didn't care. Probably the latter. Chance had told Julian plenty of horror stories over the years about domineering artistic directors. Julian knew the drill. The dance world was tough. He got it. He didn't like it, but he got it.

Then Ivanov took things too far.

"What's wrong?" he yelled at Tessa's back. Then just as she turned to face him, he blew out an angry sigh. "Are you deaf or something?"

Her eyes went as big as saucers. The color drained from her face.

The other dancers in the room all dropped their gazes to the floor. Even Chance. Even Madame Daria. No one said a word in Tessa's defense. Not one person.

Julian could feel his pulse pounding in his ears. Rage blossomed in his chest. What the hell was wrong with these people?

He stood. The backs of his knees hit the piano bench,

and it fell to the floor with a clatter. Everyone turned to look at him, including Tessa.

Chance shook his head. The message was once again unmistakable. *Stay out of it.*

But Julian couldn't. Not this time.

He didn't scream. He didn't yell. He didn't raise his voice so much as a decibel. He simply fixed his gaze with Ivanov's and said, "As a matter of fact, she is. So why don't you show some damned compassion?"

Chance sighed, and Julian could hear it from clear across the room.

"Mr. Shine!" Madame Daria shot Julian a glare that he interpreted to mean he was about to be fired.

Fine. Three days in this place was enough to drive anyone crazy. It was a miracle he'd lasted as long as he had.

Except a miracle hadn't kept Julian coming back day after day, and he knew it. Tessa had.

He glanced at her, taking in the sudden flush in her delicate cheeks and the barely perceptible tremble in her lower lip. And he realized the gravity of his mistake. It settled into his chest with a terrible, dull ache. He'd embarrassed her. He'd made things worse.

Didn't he always?

Ivanov narrowed his gaze at Julian. "What are you talking about?"

Tessa's flush deepened a few shades.

Julian cleared his throat. He wouldn't have taken the words back even if he could. Ivanov needed to know what a supreme ass he was being. If no one else would tell him, Julian was more than happy to do the honors. "You asked her if she's deaf, and the answer is yes. An apology is in order, don't you agree?"

Ivanov turned toward Tessa. "Is this true?"

She squared her shoulders and lifted her chin. "Yes, but…"

"But you decided to let your boyfriend tell me rather then letting me know when the casting sheet went up?" Ivanov crossed his arms and jerked his head in Julian's direction.

"He's not my boyfriend." Tessa seemed to be making a great effort not to look at him. "In fact, I barely know him."

Julian picked up the piano bench, slammed it back in place and began to straighten his sheet music. He pitied whoever ended up taking his place. He really did.

"You barely know him? That's about to change." The choreographer's gaze darted back and forth between the two of them before settling once again on Tessa. "Since Mr. Shine has taken such an interest in your well-being, Miss Wilde, and since you apparently have an undisclosed challenge that requires extra practice, the two of you will rehearse every evening together for an extra two hours. Is that clear?"

Julian looked up from the papers in his hand. "What? No—"

Tessa shook her head vehemently. "I don't think—"

Ivanov held up a hand, cutting both of them off. "I'm not asking. I'm telling. Either the two of you agree to this arrangement, or I choose a new pianist, as well as a new dancer for the principal role. The choice is yours."

Julian shook his head. He'd never been one to take orders, and he wasn't about to start now. Especially from a jackass like the one who'd treated Tessa so cruelly.

But apparently Tessa had other ideas.

"We'll do it."

Chapter Seven

Tessa didn't really mind staying after rehearsal for extra practice. She probably would have done so even if Ivanov hadn't insisted on it. She was preparing for her first role in a professional ballet performance. A *starring* role. She needed all the practice she could get.

But Tessa did mind the fact that she'd been reprimanded in front of the entire company. And she very much minded that the entire episode had been Julian's fault.

She didn't allow herself a single glance in his direction for the rest of rehearsal. She concentrated on memorizing the choreography and trying to tune out all the extraneous sounds in the room so she could focus on the music. It was far more difficult than she'd expected, even after the unsettling conversation she'd had with Dr. Spencer.

The dance studio was brimming with noise—Ivanov's heavily accented voice issuing corrections, the pitter-patter of ballet shoes on the studio floor, the labored breath of the dancers. Every time Tessa caught hold of the melody, something else got in the way. She could feel the music slipping through her fingers, and now that she'd heard it again, she didn't want to dance without it.

She didn't want to count the beats anymore. She just wanted to dance. Really dance.

Working alone with the piano after hours might be exactly what she needed. She could do with fewer distractions. The only problem was that the man playing the piano was the biggest distraction of all, especially now. She was furious with him.

Julian had made a spectacle out of her.

He was already bent over the upright Steinway in the smaller practice room when she walked in after rehearsal. He didn't look up. He kept pounding away on the keys until she stomped over to him and plopped her dance bag on top of the piano.

As soon as she did, the music came to an abrupt stop. Julian rested his hands on his thighs and glared at Tessa's Capezio tote. "No bags on top of the piano."

He was beyond impossible. Tessa crossed her arms and left her bag right where it was. "Why do you care? This isn't even your piano."

Besides, hadn't he made some kind of snide remark the night before about the instrument? He had. Tessa remembered his exact words.

I play piano...but it's not the same.

Julian lifted a brow. "I care because music is important to me, and this is a nice piano."

Fair point, but did he have to be so bossy? "Well, this ballet is important to me, and you almost cost me my part earlier today. What do you have to say about that, Mr. Crankypants?"

The corner of his mouth hitched up into a spontaneous grin. Then he seemed to realize he was accidentally smiling, and his expression went cool again. Neutral. "Mr. Crankypants? That's your nickname for me?"

"It suits you, don't you think?" Tessa lifted a brow. They looked at each other for a prolonged moment, until she finally plucked her bag from the piano and dropped it on the floor.

But she wasn't about to let him off the hook. "You didn't answer my question."

"About what happened earlier?" He narrowed his soulful blue eyes. If Tessa had been certain she could discern his words without having to read his lips, she would have looked away. The man was too beautiful for his own good. "I guess I'd say you're welcome."

He couldn't be serious. "If you think I'm going to thank you, you're delusional."

"Suit yourself." He shrugged and started playing again.

If Tessa concentrated very hard, she could hear each individual note and make sense of the melody. It wasn't Debussy. He was playing something different, something more fluid. Jazz. It made her want to tap her toes.

She cleared her throat. "Look, you can't do that again, okay? Promise me."

He fixed his gaze on hers, but his hands kept moving over the keys. "I can't make that promise. Sorry. The guy's a complete ass. People ought to call him out on it more often."

Tessa just stared at him, speechless. Although, why she'd expected an apology was somewhat of a mystery, given Julian's generally bizarre behavior.

Finally, she shook her head. "If you want to fight with the ballet director, be my guest. But leave me out of it. I work hard every day to try and make sure no one notices that I'm different than the rest of the dancers. You can't possibly understand what it's like."

He spoke slowly, carefully. Tessa no longer needed to read his lips to catch his meaning. "I understand more than you think I do, sweetheart."

Sweetheart.

The endearment had been infused with a heavy dose of sarcasm, but it sent a tingle coursing through her all the same. Her face went instantly hot.

She swallowed and let her gaze wander to the scar on his face. She had a sudden overwhelming urge to reach out and touch it, to let her fingertips explore the raised skin and follow its rugged trail to the corner of his mouth. What must it be like to wear your brokenness on the outside, for all the world to see? Tessa couldn't fathom it. She'd been fighting so long and so hard to hide hers.

Maybe he did understand. Just a little bit.

Julian stopped playing and signed at her. One word only. *Why?*

He was getting better at signing. Tessa wondered if

he'd been studying. She also wondered why the thought that he might have done that thrilled her as much as it did.

This is work. And you're still mad at him, remember? "Why what?"

He narrowed his gaze. "Why is this ballet so important to you? Why do you want to dance for Ivanov?"

"I'm not dancing for him. I'm dancing for me." She was still getting used to the sound of her own voice, but it was raspier now. Raw. "Is that a good enough reason?"

"It's the only good reason," he said. His expression didn't change. His mouth remained in the same flat line.

But somewhere in the depths of his moody blue eyes, Tessa spied a shadow of a smile.

Staying after hours for private practice wasn't the worst way to spend an evening. Julian was acutely aware of this fact. If he'd been in any sort of denial about it before Tessa wound the satiny ribbons of her pointe shoes around her slender ankles, he was quickly corrected.

He loved watching her dance, and now—by virtue of his own idiocy, as Tessa so kindly put it—he had a front-row seat for every lithe arabesque, every breathtaking twirl.

He tried not to stare. He tried really damn hard.

Even without Daria there to monitor her *no ogling* rule, it didn't seem appropriate. But he couldn't stop himself. He began each round focused intently on the keys in front of him, but before Tessa was halfway through her combination, he was playing the music by rote while he watched her every move.

There was a purity in the way her body floated across the floor. An aching honesty that made Julian's chest grow tight, especially during the adagio portions of the music. Debussy's composition, with its glittering restraint and absence of traditional tonality, was the perfect backdrop for her artistry. As much as Julian loved music—as much as he'd lived and breathed it for the majority of his life—it was reduced to nothing more than background noise as Tessa danced. Sometimes he didn't even hear it. It somehow fell away while she told a story with her lyrical arms and the sweeping turns of her pink-slippered feet.

She was so intent on blending in with the rest of the dancers. She never would. As far as Julian was concerned, that's what made Tessa so special. He couldn't shake her words from earlier.

I'm not dancing for him. I'm dancing for me.

Julian couldn't help but wonder if dance had become her way of communicating in a world that had suddenly gone silent. If so, despite his efforts not to, he was hanging on to her every word.

But then something happened that gave him pause.

He might never have noticed it, if not for the metronome.

"Why do you have that?" Tessa asked as he pulled the device from his messenger bag and set it on top of the piano. "You just casually carry a metronome around wherever you go?"

"Maybe." Of course he didn't.

He'd spent nearly an hour looking for it in his apartment, after he'd read the article on nonauditory cues for deaf dancers that he'd told Chance about. It was just a regular metronome, nothing fancy. A Wittner, with a wind-up spring and a swinging pendulum that rocked back and forth, in time with the beat. But it should do the trick.

He picked it up and wound the crank. "I thought it might be useful."

Tessa watched as he placed it back on the piano and the pendulum ticked to and fro. "So this was your idea?"

He shrugged. "I might have read something somewhere about visual cues for dancers with hearing impairments."

She stared at him for six long clicks of the metronome before finally saying something. "That's very thoughtful of you, Julian."

He broke his gaze and played a chord, a wistful E minor. Tessa spoke through her dance, and Julian spoke best through his music. They had more in common than he'd realized.

He glanced up. She was looking at him more closely than he felt comfortable with, especially when her gaze lingered so long on his scar. Maybe she was just reading his lips. It was hard to tell. "It's nothing. Are you ready?"

She nodded and adjusted the wraparound sweater she wore over her leotard as she glided her way back to the center of the floor.

Julian waited until she struck her beginning pose and nodded to hit the opening note of the Debussy piece. He played each successive part of the melody with care, moving in perfect time with the metronome's swinging arm.

Tessa glanced at it every few beats and seemed to be suppressing a smile. Julian was suddenly very glad that Chance was nowhere around to read more into the situation.

Is there more?

Julian's jaw clenched.

No, there wasn't. He was helping her…under duress now. That was it. Neither of them was particularly happy about it, tolerable though it might be.

Halfway through her solo, it happened.

Julian caught himself watching Tessa when he should have been concentrating on his music. Again. He cursed under his breath, but in the split second before he refocused on the piano keys, he noticed that she was off the beat. Her feet were moving too fast. Her count was probably a half second ahead of the metronome's steady click, which wouldn't have seemed exceedingly odd, except for one thing—Julian was also off.

He'd gotten ahead of the beat as well, probably because he'd slipped and let himself get lost in Tessa's dance, when he should have been focusing on his playing. The fact that he was so out of practice probably hadn't helped, but that didn't seem to matter at the moment.

As he slowed the tempo of the music, Tessa's movements slowed, as well. Even as he changed tempo, she stayed perfectly in sync with him. Note for note. Beat for beat.

She can hear me.

No. That wasn't possible. Tessa was deaf. It had to

be a coincidence, or something else. There had to be a sensible explanation. Maybe she could feel the piano's vibration in the soles of her feet. That had to be it.

Except the music hadn't even reached its swell. Julian was barely touching the keys, stretching out the adagio, letting the silence speak as much as the song.

They remained in perfect sync. Ignored, the metronome ticked away.

Mind reeling, Julian played on. As the music grew, billowing around them, so did his recollection of the ill-fated lift. It started with Tessa's panic, and then the near fall. Without even realizing it, Julian had stopped playing. Ivanov's tirade had followed.

Are you deaf or something?

Julian's blood began to boil again just thinking about it. Of course he'd said something. He'd had to. But not right away…he'd done something first, hadn't he?

He'd stood up.

When he did, the piano bench had fallen to the floor. It made a terrible racket, as falling furniture was wont to do. Suddenly, Julian hadn't been the invisible guy in the corner. Everyone in the room flinched and then turned to look at him.

Everyone, including Tessa.

Had she heard something then?

Could she hear his music *now*?

The signs all pointed to the same conclusion—yes.

But it didn't make sense. Tessa was deaf. She'd fallen and hit her head. Julian highly doubted she'd been faking her injury for more than a year.

He must be mistaken. Julian didn't know the first

thing about being deaf. He'd done a bit of research lately, but that didn't make him an expert. Far from it.

Julian knew music, though. He knew harmony, melody and rhythm. He knew sound. And despite her mysterious fragility, Tessa was suddenly looking more and more like a woman who could hear.

By the time she finished her run-through, they'd clocked two hours of extra practice, enough to satisfy Ivanov. Between company class, rehearsal and the evening with Tessa, Julian had been playing for ten hours, with only a few small breaks here and there. Mentally, he was drained. But physically, he felt pretty good. Relaxed. Fluid. He hadn't felt so loose in as long as he could remember.

He kept playing the piano while Tessa unwound the ribbons from her ankles and slipped out of her ballet shoes. Just a little free-form jazz. Soon it progressed into a familiar tune, one he used to play on his trumpet— "La Vie en Rose." Louis Armstrong's version, naturally.

Julian had no doubt found his way to that particular song by virtue of Tessa's pink tights and pink satin shoes. "La Vie en Rose"—"Life in Rosy Hues." It made sense. He'd been neck-deep in pink for three days running. But after he made his way through the prelude, the song's lyrics floated to the forefront of his mind.

Armstrong hadn't been singing about a color. He'd been singing about a woman. He'd been singing about what it felt like to hold her close and fast, to kiss her until heaven sighed. Until life took on a rosy hue.

Julian abruptly stopped playing.

He jammed a shaky hand through his hair and then

focused on packing away the metronome and gathering his things together, while Tessa did the same.

"Thank you for staying," she said as she rose to her feet and closed the distance between them. "I think it helped. I've got the combination down now."

"Okay, then. Good." He gave her a curt nod. It wasn't as though he'd had a choice in the matter.

Julian was very ready to leave all of a sudden. But he wasn't about to leave Tessa alone in the building, so he followed her out of the practice room and down the darkened hallway.

She paused near the door to the rehearsal space. "I think I left my coat in here earlier."

Fall was nipping at New York's heels. Leaves were already swirling in the air, and Central Park was blanketed with red-and-yellow foliage. She'd freeze without her coat this time of night.

Julian tried the doorknob and found the room unlocked. He pushed the door open. "After you."

She slid past him, and Julian did his best to ignore the way his body hardened as her shoulder grazed his chest. It was just the barest of contact, but it was enough.

More than enough.

He blamed his overactive libido on the fact that he'd been a hermit for the better part of two years.

He hadn't always been so solitary. There'd been women in his life before the accident. A lot of women. Sometimes more than one in a night, in his less gentlemanly moments.

Julian hated to think about it now. Not just the

women, but everything else, too—the partying, the long nights on the road, the money. So much money.

He'd been at the top of his game. He'd been the best trumpet player in the country, if not the world.

He'd give anything to get those days back. Or even just one of them…a single day, which he'd spend immersed in his music from morning to night.

The root of his bitterness wasn't the accident. It never had been. The reason he was so angry was because he deserved what had happened to him. He'd forgotten the only thing that mattered—the music.

He'd gotten caught up in the trappings and turned his back on everything he believed in. He'd tempted fate, and fate had paid him back in spades.

Things were different with Tessa, though, and he didn't know why. Even after so much time alone, there was absolutely no reason why he should feel this way about a woman he barely knew. A woman he had no business pursuing. A woman he *wouldn't* pursue.

He was darkness.

She was light.

But that didn't stop him from wanting her.

Julian cleared his throat and averted his gaze from her slender, elegant frame. She moved with such eloquence, even when she was simply walking across the room. But the dance studio was covered in mirrors, from floor to ceiling, and there was nowhere safe to look.

Tessa was everywhere.

He inhaled a tense breath and somehow spotted a flash of yellow out of the corner of his eye. A coat, slung over the ballet barre.

He picked it up. It looked just like the sort of thing she would wear. Cheery and bright, like a daisy. "I don't suppose this is it?"

Tessa turned her head. "It is. Thank you."

She'd either heard him, or she'd had her eyes trained on his reflection. Specifically, on his mouth. The possibility did little to minimize his erection.

He held the coat open for her, as much to shield himself as to help her into it. When Tessa reached him, she turned to slide her arms into the sleeves, and his gaze lingered on the graceful curve of her neck.

God, she was beautiful. Like a perfect, precious pearl. Her hair was still swept into a ballerina bun, and it shimmered like a copper penny beneath the moonlight streaming through the studio's high-placed windows. Julian was practically spellbound by a stray curl that had escaped her updo and rested in a gentle swirl on her alabaster shoulder.

Tessa dipped her head to button her coat, and Julian knew it was time for him to step away. But he couldn't seem to make his feet move. If anything, he leaned a fraction closer, drawn to her like gravity.

It occurred to him he could say anything to her right then. He could confess the worst of his sins, his darkest secrets, and she'd never know.

Unless he was right, and she could actually hear.

He wanted to know. More than wanted, truthfully. He *needed* to know. All it would take was one tiny whisper. Just a single word. A test, of sorts.

Don't.

He knew damn well he shouldn't do it. But he also

knew he would. The temptation was too great, but the stakes were too tantalizingly high. He leaned a fraction closer and murmured the first thing that came to mind...the words he'd been struggling for the hours, for days, not to say.

"Kiss me, Tessa."

Chapter Eight

Kiss me, Tessa.

She heard it as clear as day, just over her right shoulder. There was no mistaking the fevered longing in Julian's voice. The *ache*. Even if Tessa had been imagining things, even if she'd somehow conjured the whispered command by wishing very hard, it would have never sounded like that. So decadent. So deliciously dark.

She spun her head around before she could stop herself.

Julian didn't even look surprised. His sapphire gaze burned into her, all knowing, all seeing. With a barely perceptible smile and one arched brow, he seemed more satisfied than shocked.

He knew she could hear. Had he known it all along? But then his gaze dropped to her mouth, and she saw something else in the depths of those discerning eyes.

Intention.

Kiss me, Tessa.

He didn't say it again. He didn't need to. The air around them was thick with those words. Tessa could still hear them whirling in her mind like a favorite song. They rang like a melody that somehow expressed everything her heart was screaming to say when she'd been too shy, too afraid to speak.

The way he was looking at her mouth made her feel a little bit wicked. She hadn't felt that way in a very long time, if ever. And she liked it. She liked it a lot.

Her lips parted, and she rose up on tiptoe, but before she could do as he'd said and kiss him, Julian groaned and claimed her mouth with his.

At once, she was flooded with sensation—the hard press of the ballet barre against the small of her back as Julian leaned into her, the sound of her heart beating wildly in her ears, as if she'd just done a series of *fouetté* turns, and the fierce hunger of Julian's kiss... the taste of him, warm and wonderful, like brandy on a snowy night.

Tessa had never been kissed like this before. Ever. It made her head spin, and it made her do other things, too. Things she'd never imagined herself doing, like whimpering helplessly into Julian's mouth and clawing at his back until the fabric of his grey dress shirt was balled in her fists.

Julian's hands were suddenly in her hair, untangling her ballerina bun, and his body—hard...so very, very hard—was pressed against her, hemming her in. Somewhere in the back of her mind, beneath the delirious haze of arousal, she was aware of a profound shift taking place. A wall coming down.

Since the moment she'd fallen a year ago and lost her hearing, she'd felt as if she'd been living on the outside of things. She could still talk, obviously, and she could read lips to communicate. But the silence was always there, an invisible obstacle between Tessa and everyone else.

At first, she'd railed against it. But then Owen had given voice to her worst fears and told her he no longer felt close to her. He'd walked away, all because she could no longer hear. Afterward, she'd embraced the silence. She'd used it as a barrier to protect herself from being hurt again. From falling.

As Julian deepened the kiss, slanting his mouth over hers and grinding his erection against her center, she felt like a participant in her life again, rather than an observer. No longer on the outside. She was at the center of her world. Not just *her* world. *The* world. The center of everything.

She let her hands slide lower, and lower still, until they were on Julian's hips, pulling him more firmly against her. Now that the wall had come down, she needed more. More sound, more sensation, more life. More of *him*—this astonishing, enigmatic man who'd found a way through.

"Julian," she whispered as he dipped his head to kiss the hollow of her throat. If she'd been able to think straight—if she'd been able to think *at all*—she might have been embarrassed. Surely he could feel the frantic beat of her pulse beneath his lips. He could taste the effect he had on her.

But what did it matter? He knew, anyway. He'd probably known that she felt drawn to him from the moment she'd first seen him, beautiful and brooding, in the train station. He seemed to know everything else about her. There was no sense in hiding.

She didn't want to hide anymore. Not from him, and not from the desire that was flowing through her, making her shiver all over.

"Yes, love?" he murmured.

God, that sound…his voice. Hearing it felt almost as good as an actual caress. Almost…

"Touch me," she said, letting her coat slip off her shoulders and fall to the floor, before reaching for the tie of her wraparound sweater.

Her hands shook so much that she couldn't unfasten the bow. Julian tipped her chin upward and kissed her— softly, slowly this time—and he took over, untying her sweater and peeling it away, along with her leotard. The air was shockingly cold on her exposed breasts.

Tessa inhaled a shuddering breath as Julian looked at her. Then he lifted his gaze to hers and held up his hand, palm forward, with all five fingers up in the air. His blue eyes glittered in the darkness, and he moved his hand in a circular motion over his face. He was talking to her again with his hands. Signing.

Beautiful.

A lump lodged in Tessa's throat, and she reached for him, cupping his face in her hands and drawing the pad of her thumb across his skillful mouth. Just as she made contact with the scar tissue on his face, Julian caught her wrist in his grasp and gently placed her hand on the ballet barre. He did the same with her other hand and held them both in place, his musical fingers circling her wrists like bracelets.

Then he kissed his way down the curve of her neck and across her collarbone, until his mouth was on her breast, and the chill that had hit her so hard and fast was replaced with the searing heat of Julian's lips, the wet relief of his tongue.

Oh, God.

Tessa's eyes drifted closed. The last thing she saw before she gave herself up to Julian's touch and the beckoning darkness was her mirrored reflection. Languidly arched against the barre, heavy lidded and breathless, while Julian pleasured her with his mouth.

She didn't look at all like herself. Such a provocative image. It would no doubt be burned into her memory from here on out. She was sure to remember it every time she stood in that spot, pointing her toes and going through her daily ballet exercises.

Plié, élevé, dégagé.

It was almost like signing—speaking without words, using her body to communicate. Tessa had been a dancer all her life. Like most ballerinas, she thought of her body as a tool. But right then, it felt like more. So much more.

With her eyes shut, everything began moving in a blur of quickened breaths and rapid heartbeats. Julian's hands were everywhere, and Tessa felt like she was on fire. Molten. Burning from the inside out.

Her knees buckled, and Julian lowered her to the studio floor. She was barely aware of the wood beneath her. It seemed as if every nerve ending in her body was reaching for Julian, seeking his touch, his kiss... his everything.

She tugged at his shirt, but her limbs had gone so pleasantly limp that her efforts were ineffective. Julian gathered her wrists in his hands again and pinned her arms over her head while he carefully finished undressing her. And then she was completely bare, right there in the ballet studio. It was such an inconceivable idea, that if Tessa would have thought about it, she wouldn't have believed it.

But she didn't want to think anymore. She just wanted to experience the moment with him. She wanted to be connected to another person for once. How had she gone so long without it? Without *this*?

"Look at me, Tessa," he murmured against her ear, and she felt the low scrape of his voice as much as she heard it.

Her eyes fluttered open. Julian loomed over her with his hands planted on either side of her head.

"You're beautiful." This time he said it instead of signing it. Tessa watched his mouth form the words, captivated by the shape of his lips and the jagged scar beside them. He had the most exquisite mouth she'd ever seen. Mysterious. A mouth full of secrets.

"So are you," she said, and she meant every word.

Julian's eyes went as dark as sapphires. He lowered his head, and that lovely mouth of his made a trail straight down the middle of her body, starting at the base of her throat, moving slowly, deliberately, down her breastbone, until his five o'clock shadow grazed the tender skin on her belly.

Tessa took a sharp, shuddering inhale, as she realized he'd also begun to move his fingertips up the inside of her thigh. She'd wanted more, and he was giving it to her. But it was almost too much. She couldn't catch her breath, and the heat swirling through her body was suddenly concentrated between her legs.

Her hips rose off the floor, seeking relief, and Julian kissed her again. In the most intimate way possible.

Tessa buried her hands in Julian's hair, and somewhere in her consciousness, she was aware that she was writhing beneath him, crying his name.

This, she thought. *This is what it means to let someone inside.* She'd wanted connection. Once she'd realized he wanted it, too, she'd craved it. But she'd been wholly unprepared for how overwhelming it would feel. How blissful. How exquisitely vulnerable.

"Yes," she whimpered.

Julian's mouth moved faster, kissing, licking, tasting, and just when she thought the pleasure might kill her, he slipped a finger inside her, and she shattered.

Her climax hit hard and fast. She felt like she was blossoming from the very center of her body, unfolding in Julian's hands. Still he stroked her, kissing the sensitive inside of her thigh and moving his magic, musical fingers inside and out, prolonging her orgasm, until she had nothing left to give.

Like a piece of music drifting toward the coda after its swell.

* * *

It was supposed to be a kiss. Just an innocent kiss. It wasn't supposed to go any further than that.

But when Julian's lips had first touched Tessa's, he'd known he was in trouble. She was so responsive, so *willing*, that he'd lost his head. He'd forgotten all the reasons that touching her was a bad idea and lost himself in the sweetness of her, in the thrill of sharing her light.

He wanted to make her feel good. He wanted to make her *feel*. To let go like she never had before.

When she came apart, it was the most dazzling thing he'd ever seen. While she still pulsed against his hand, he lifted his head to look at her face, and it wasn't her seductively parted lips or her heavily lidded eyes that captivated him so.

Rather, it was her astonished expression that made his heart feel like it was being squeezed in a vise. She'd opened up for him, and he'd shown her a part of herself that she hadn't known existed. A beautiful, vulnerable part that was so damned desirable, it brought Julian to his knees.

Then he made the mistake of taking his eyes off her…just for a fraction of a second. But it was long enough to catch a glimpse of his reflection in the studio mirrors. Long enough to see the scar on his face and remember.

"I want you, Julian." Tessa rose up on her knees and reached for him, placing her hand on his fly and the swell of his erection.

Starlight streamed through windows overhead, bathing her lithe body in pale, shimmering light, and she looked almost too beautiful to be real. He throbbed beneath her touch, and it would have been so easy to take her right then, right there. He wanted her more than he wanted to take his next breath.

But it wasn't that simple. Not anymore. He wasn't the old Julian, and his face wasn't the only part of him that was scarred.

Maybe if he hadn't been surrounded on every side by his reflection, he could have gone through with it. They could have properly finished what they'd started. But he couldn't seem to ignore all those godforsaken mirrors.

I want you, Julian.

She didn't know what she was saying.

"Babe, we…" *We can't. I can't. Not here.*

Tessa kissed him before he could get the rest of the words out. And for a moment, he nearly forgot again. He closed his eyes and groaned while she caressed him over his trousers. Her hand on his erection was almost unbearable. He couldn't stop now…it seemed impossible. Not when she was right there, in his arms, offering herself to him. So gloriously naked.

Her body was perfect—long and lean from years of ballet, and as strong as it was supple. Like a marble statue come to life, something Michelangelo had created, all gently sloping curves and Renaissance femininity.

It was that perfection that brought him back from the brink. Tessa slid her hand from his fly to his shirt, unfastened the top button and then moved to the next. Julian looked down at her beautiful breasts and delicate nipples, as soft and pink as ballet slippers, and he caught her wrist to stop her.

He could have avoided the shirt altogether, unzipped his fly and taken her without getting undressed. He thought about it. He'd been thinking about doing that very thing for days, truth be told. But it seemed wrong. He'd already committed enough sins tonight, and it was too late, anyway. Tessa was already peering up at him with questions shining in her eyes. Questions he didn't want to answer.

He shook his head. "No."

The confusion in her gaze melted into something else, something that made Julian feel more like a monster than he ever had before. Her eyes were filled with hurt, brimming with shiny, unshed tears.

"No?" She blinked. Then she said it again, louder and dripping with incredulity. *"No?"*

A dullness took root in Julian's chest. It was the exact opposite of the arousal he'd been drowning in just moments before. This was all his fault…that look in her eyes, the shame and embarrassment in her voice…all of it.

He held up his hands in a gesture of surrender. "Tessa."

It was too little, too late.

"Stop," she said. She signed the word at the same time, holding out her left palm and bringing her right hand down on it at a right angle, as if slicing something in two.

The meaning of the gesture wasn't lost on Julian. He'd screwed up, and now whatever tenuous connection they had was broken.

Tessa's gaze dropped to her bare breasts, and her

cheeks flamed pink in the darkness. She stood and began scrambling back into her clothes. Julian tried to help, and she pushed his hands away. He could only stand and watch while she turned her back and finished getting dressed.

"I'm sorry," he said. When she didn't acknowledge him, he said it again, louder, uncertain just how much she could hear. "I'm sorry."

Tessa covered her ears with her hands and shook her head.

She could hear him, all right.

She just didn't want to listen.

Chapter Nine

Tessa woke up the next morning, and the shame she'd felt the night before came crashing down on her again the second she opened her eyes.

She'd never been so mortified in her life.

Julian's way of letting her know that he'd figured out she could hear had been to demand that she kiss him. Like an idiot, she obeyed. She hadn't even explained how or why she could hear him. Then somehow she'd ended up naked on the studio floor, trembling from her very first orgasm.

As if that wasn't bad enough, she'd all but begged him to have sex with her, and he'd stopped her. He'd *rejected* her. After playing her body like an instrument, he was finished. Done. No explanation, no string of words at all.

Just *no*.

She'd been completely exposed, and he hadn't shed a single article of clothing. His forest green tie with the tiny white polka dots had hardly been crooked. Tessa had been forced to fumble her way back into her dance clothes while he stood there watching.

She'd wanted to die.

Just thinking about it made her want to die all over again. It also made her want to grab hold of Julian's fancy, Sinatra-esque tie and strangle him with it.

She sighed. Long and loud. How could she show her face at rehearsal today? How could she stand at the barre in the exact spot where he'd kissed her silly, while he pounded away on the piano in the corner of the room?

And *how on earth* was she going to survive practicing with him after hours?

"Mr. B, I've made a huge mistake," she muttered. "The hugest."

The dog always slept at the foot of her bed. He must have sensed something was wrong, because he'd spent the night with his little furry body tucked into the crook of her neck. At the sound of Tessa's voice, he lifted his head and licked the side of her face.

As sweet as Mr. B's intentions had likely been, the sleeping situation was less than ideal. Tessa now had a stiff neck, in addition to her very wounded pride. She sat up and moved her head from side to side, wincing in pain.

She wasn't even out of bed yet and already the day was a disaster. Perfect.

Tessa tossed off the covers, grabbed a leotard and tights from her dresser and pulled them on, trying her hardest not to think about the last time she'd gone through the same ritual. It was no use. Everything about the night before was burned permanently into her consciousness. She couldn't forget a thing about it if she'd tried.

Oh, how she tried.

"I'll teach the early-morning class today," she said as she walked into the kitchen of the Wilde family brownstone and poured herself a giant cup of coffee.

Her mother glanced up from the table, where a stack of invoices, a checkbook and several spreadsheets sat in front of her. "Good morning. Are you sure you want to teach? Don't you have rehearsal today?"

Tessa sipped her coffee and reminded herself to read her mother's lips when she spoke, even though the kitchen was quiet enough for her to make sense of what she was hearing.

Her mom sounded different than she did before Tessa's accident. Older. The fall had taken its toll on everyone.

Tessa swallowed. She hated not telling her mother that she might be getting her hearing back for good. If she did, though, her mother would insist on talking to Dr. Spencer, and then Tessa would have to battle both of them to keep her part in the ballet.

She'd tell her family after opening night. It was only three weeks away. By then, everything would be fine.

"Rehearsal doesn't start until ten. Let me take the first class. Adult beginner ballet, right? It'll be fun." Fun was a stretch, but it would definitely be a distraction, and that's precisely what Tessa needed.

Every time she closed her eyes, she saw Julian gazing down at her with those blazing blue eyes of his. She saw his hand fanning in a circle around his face, signing.

Beautiful.

"Are you feeling okay?" Her mother frowned. "Your face is flushed."

Tessa cleared her throat. "I'm fine."

She was *not* fine.

Her mother's gaze narrowed. "You got in awfully late last night. How many hours a day does Ivanov have you rehearsing?"

"I stayed late to go over a few things. I'll probably do the same again tonight." Tessa pasted on a smile. She'd already planned to do everything in her power to get out of private rehearsal tonight. At the very least, she could make sure she wasn't alone with Julian. That couldn't happen again.

She couldn't kiss him again. *Ever.* And she'd obviously be keeping her clothes on from here on out.

A thrill of remembrance coursed through her, following quickly by a pang of humiliation. He'd seen her at her most vulnerable. He'd done things to her that no man had ever done before. Did he have any idea how difficult it was for her to let down her guard like that?

Clearly not.

She certainly wouldn't make that mistake again. Lesson learned.

She sipped her coffee, relishing the way it burned as it went down. Black and bitter, like her mood. She wanted to stay angry for as long as possible, because the alternative seemed to be to feel crushed. He'd turned her down after all.

Why? What was wrong with her?

She swallowed. Hard. Despite the indignity of what happened, she couldn't shake the feeling that the real reason had had nothing whatsoever to do with her.

He'd wanted her. She hadn't been wrong about that. She'd seen the desire in the eyes from the moment she'd turned around after he'd whispered in her ear.

Kiss me, Tessa.

Arousal had rolled off him in waves…in every lingering glance, every caress, every decadent brush of his fingertips. He'd been as hard as granite.

For her.

"Tessa, I'm worried about you. Are you absolutely certain dancing with the company isn't taking a toll on you?" Her mother pushed back from the table and crossed her arms.

Now that she was a member of the company, Tessa should probably start thinking about moving into her own apartment again. The three-story Brooklyn walk-up where she'd lived for three years before her accident had been like a slice of heaven. Her own little piece of the Big Apple. But she'd needed help adjusting to life after her injury, so she'd moved back into the family brownstone. It was a safe haven that had belonged to the Wildes for three generations. The prewar building was adorned with limestone and granite columns and boasted an exclusive address on Riverside Drive. Even Zander still lived there…technically. He'd pretty much moved into the penthouse suite at the Bennington when he took over as CEO.

Tessa took another fortifying gulp of coffee. She'd have to somehow make it to opening night before she thought about moving. "Mom, this is all I've wanted for my entire life. Try to be happy for me, okay?"

Once upon a time, a dance career had been what her mother wanted, too. But after only a year as a corps dancer, Emily had become pregnant with Zander. She'd quit dancing professionally and never went back. The Wilde School of Dance was born shortly after Zander.

As far as Tessa could tell, her mother never regretted her decision. She loved being a mother. She loved running a dance school. When Tessa's father passed away at the young age of forty, from a congenital heart defect, his death seemed to confirm that Emily had done the right thing. If she'd gone back to dancing, she might have been traveling the world, rather than teaching during the day and coming home to her family every night. She might not have even been there when Tessa's father collapsed and had to be taken to the hospital.

Tessa understood all of this. But there was a very important difference between her and her mother—quitting had been Emily's choice. Her decision. On the day thirteen months ago, when Owen dropped her and her head hit the ground, her power to choose suffered a blow, as well. She'd been fighting to get it back ever since.

"I'm thrilled for you, darling. You know that," Emily said.

Tessa nodded, although she wasn't sure her mother was telling the truth, the whole truth and nothing but the truth. "I know, and I'm serious about class this morning. I realize you've been shorthanded since I joined the company."

Emily smiled. "If you insist. Thank you, darling. You know you'll always have a place at the Wilde School of Dance."

"I know, Mom." Tessa filled a travel mug with coffee and fastened Mr. B's leash onto his collar.

"Always," her mother said again, as Tessa headed out the door.

As if Tessa could forget about the grand backup plan.

She knew she should consider herself lucky. She had a roof over her head, a family that loved her and a job waiting for her if things at the company went south. Plus she was teetering on the verge of a medical miracle.

She wanted to dance, though. Right or wrong, she wanted more.

More.

That's what she'd wanted last night, too. From Julian.

And look what a disaster that had been.

Julian was furious with himself for allowing things to spiral so out of control the night before. So furious that he seriously considered not showing up for rehearsal and quitting his job altogether, but that didn't seem right. It was the coward's way out.

At ten o'clock sharp, he was seated at the piano, going through the scales, while the dancers drifted into the studio, taking their places at the barre. He couldn't quite chalk up his attendance to a sense of honor, though. Julian had already proven himself to be most dishonorable. The truth of the matter was he couldn't stay away. Not from the mess he'd created, and not from Tessa.

She could hear.

In the fevered heat of what had followed that startling revelation, they hadn't discussed it. Not a single word.

He was curious as hell. How? *When?* Did anyone else know? He seriously doubted it. But why the secrecy?

Questions spun through his mind as his hands moved instinctively over the keys. He played a D chord, followed by E flat, F, G, A, B, C and D. A classic jazz Dorian modal scale. He improvised a little with his right hand. A few of the dancers glanced his direction, including Chance.

Chance nodded and smiled, no doubt convinced Julian was composing something for Zander Wilde's The Circle Club at the Bennington.

Julian shook his head. *Think again.*

He was just messing around. Besides, if he were ever going to play at a jazz club, he wouldn't write something ahead of time. He'd do it right. Jazz wasn't about composing. By its very nature, jazz was about improvisation. That's what Julian loved most about jazz. It was a creative whirlwind, new and different every time. An extemporaneous poem.

Not that he'd given any thought to The Circle Club. Because he hadn't. He'd made a serious ongoing effort *not* to think about it.

In that regard, his regret over the night before had been almost convenient. It had certainly kept any stray visions of himself seated at the glossy grand piano at the Bennington from creeping into his thoughts. There wasn't room in his head for anything but the memory of Tessa's lips, her balletic limbs, her slender hips rising and falling beneath his touch, wanting…seeking. More.

More of him.

Julian's hand slipped, and a jarring off-key note resonated from the piano. Tessa strode into the studio just in time to witness his mistake. Assuming she could hear it.

Julian's gaze followed her as she walked across the room. She moved with purpose, back ramrod straight and chin defiantly lifted. She stopped at her usual place at the barre—the same spot where he'd kissed her before she'd untied her wraparound sweater and pleaded with him. *Touch me.*

Tessa lingered for a moment and then squared her shoulders and moved to a different spot, clear on the other side of studio. Her gaze never strayed toward Julian. Not once.

Message received.

They were going to pretend nothing had happened. She was going to ignore him completely. Before long, the memory of their near lovemaking would be erased entirely. Life goes on.

Julian banged out another chord on the piano. *Fine.*

Except it wasn't fine. He'd never forget.

"Let's get started, everyone." Madame Daria stood at the center of the room and clapped her hands.

A hush fell over the room as the dancers all turned to face the same direction, with one hand resting gently on the barre and feet turned out in first position. Daria nodded at Julian, and he launched into something classical, with a steady beat, appropriate for a full barre exercise.

Of course for Julian, *steady* meant boring as hell. He entertained himself by continuing to not think about The Circle Club and willing his memory not to stray to last night with Tessa. But he kept catching himself watching Tessa, searching for signals that she could hear.

The signs were subtle, imperceptible almost, but Julian found them. If he could see it, so could everyone else. She needed to be careful, or pretty soon he wouldn't be the only one who knew her secret.

Not your problem.

True. It was Tessa's. And the delicate, gossamer thread that had somehow seemed to tie them to one another was gone now. Broken. By *his* choice.

So Julian should have been glad when rehearsal ended and he moved to the smaller, after-hours practice room and found Chance circling the floor in a *tour jeté*. Julian should have been delighted. He should have been freaking jumping for joy.

Be careful what you wish for.

A spike of irritation hit him hard in the gut. He tossed his messenger bag on the floor, beside the piano bench, and met Chance's gaze in the mirror. "What are you doing here?"

Chance turned toward Julian and planted his hands on his hips. "Excuse me?"

Julian cleared his throat. "Sorry. I just didn't expect to find you here after hours. I thought you had a policy against this sort of thing."

"I do." Chance shrugged. "But Tessa asked me to stay."

"Did she, now?" Interesting.

Chance's brow furrowed. "She's my partner now, remember?"

"Of course I remember." Julian's voice had an unintentional edge to it.

Whether he wanted to admit it or not, part of him had been looking forward to being alone with Tessa tonight. She despised him now, with good reason. But on some level, he'd thought once they were alone together, she could forgive him. Or at least look at him.

With Chance there, she'd have no reason to acknowledge his presence.

Suck it up. This is what you deserve.

"Is there a problem?" Chance asked.

The door opened, and Tessa walked in.

Julian shook his head to indicate that no, there wasn't a problem. If there was, he certainly wasn't going to discuss it in front of Tessa.

But Chance wasn't going to let things go so easily. Did he ever?

Tessa said hello, walked to the barre and began rummaging through her bag. She sat on the floor with her back to Julian and began the complicated process of slipping on her pointe shoes and winding the long pink ribbons around her slender ankles.

Chance moved slightly so he was out of her line of vision and said, "If there's no problem, then why are you looking at me like that?"

Behind him, Tessa went still.

Chance held up his hands in a gesture of surrender. "She's off-limits. I get that. You know I'd rather not be here."

Shit. "Stop," Julian said through clenched teeth.

Chance shrugged. "Don't worry. She can't hear me, remember?"

But she could. The way the pink ribbons had begun to tremble in her hands was a clear indication that she knew exactly what was going on.

"Why are you glaring at me like that? This is what you wanted. You asked me to help her. Does 'nonauditory cues' ring a bell? Here I am. I'm doing this for you."

Tessa's gaze met Julian's in the mirror.

He swallowed and redirected his attention at Chance. "Got it. Let's just get started."

Chance let out a long, weary sigh.

Julian sat and played a few notes in an attempt to move things along, but Tessa still wasn't finished with her shoes, and Chance was looking at him with the same meddlesome expression he'd had at the Bennington when Tessa had walked into the lobby and so clearly taken Julian's breath away.

"Just ask her out. You know you want to." Chance was standing right beside the piano now, and he'd lowered his voice. Julian had no idea if Tessa could still hear him. But if Chance didn't stop, Julian was going to pummel him. "Is it the burns? The scars aren't as bad as you think they are. I promise, man. No one's going to run screaming if you take your shirt off."

And there it was.

Chance had never directly mentioned Julian's burns before. Not since Julian had been declared healed and released from his doctor's care. He'd been tiptoeing around the topic for a long time, and at last he'd decided to tackle it head-on.

Right there, in right in front of Tessa.

Julian closed his eyes. Physically, he was as healthy as he was going to get. But he was a long way from being healed. Chance was only trying to help, just like he always did. This time, he'd gone too far.

Julian's only hope was that Tessa hadn't heard. His throat was bone-dry. He wanted to say something. Anything. But he couldn't form words. He couldn't even swallow.

She didn't hear.

She didn't.

But when he opened his eyes, the look on her face said it all. As much as it had pained Julian to see the hurt in her bottomless green eyes, the brimming, unshed tears when he'd told her no, there was one thing he'd have hated to see there more. It was there now, looking back at him in the dance-studio mirror.

Pity.

Chapter Ten

"Julian Shine won't return my calls." Zander arched a single eyebrow and crossed his arms, flashing a pair of cuff links that probably cost more than what Tessa made in a month. Maybe in a year. Frustration rolled off him in waves.

Tessa loved her brother, and she was immensely proud of all that he'd accomplished. At just under thirty, he was one of the youngest—if not *the* youngest—self-made billionaires in Manhattan. But every so often, he drove her nuts.

Now was one of those times.

"You felt the need to come all the way down here to tell me that?" Tessa glanced at the clock above her mother's vintage record player. "At eight thirty in the morning?"

She hadn't even finished her coffee. Tessa had barely

had time to unlock the Wilde School of Dance's doors
and flip on the lights before Zander turned up, asking
for help.

Except technically, he hadn't asked. In true alpha-
male fashion, he'd announced his problem and then
stood there waiting for Tessa to fix it.

"This is important, and now seems to be the only
time you're free. Mom says you're at rehearsal from
morning to night, every day." He sighed and bent to
give Mr. B a pat on the head. "She's worried about
you, you know."

"Yes, I know. But things are fine. They're more than
fine. I'm dancing the lead, remember? Things are great."

Things were not actually great. Things were complicated, and they seemed to be growing more complicated
by the day. Case in point: her brother was apparently
here to discuss Julian.

Call her crazy, but Tessa wasn't exactly keen on chatting up her brother about the man she'd nearly had sex
with on the ballet-studio floor a week ago. Especially
since she'd barely exchanged two words with Julian in
the week following that mortifying, yet thoroughly delicious, experience.

She wasn't angry with him anymore. Not completely.
It had been pretty easy to figure out why Julian had
stopped things when he had once she overheard the
conversation between him and Chance.

*Is it the burns? The scars aren't as bad as you think
they are.*

The scars.

Tessa couldn't stop thinking about them…about *him*.

She wanted to talk to him, to tell him she wasn't afraid of whatever he was trying to hide. Maybe she should be, but she wasn't. She knew what it was like to transform into a different person in the blink of an eye. Tragedies changed people. If anyone could understand that, Tessa could.

But Julian had barely looked at her in the week since that night. Oh, how the tables had turned.

"The role is a big responsibility. I've been practicing after hours. It's no big deal." Tessa shrugged.

The evening rehearsals were the bane of her existence. She spent the entire two hours every night doing her best to focus on Chance and their *pas de deux* instead of seeking out Julian's reflection in the mirrored walls. She'd caught him watching her more than once. But he always packed up his messenger bag and left before she could catch him for a private conversation.

"And now you're teaching here every morning." Zander stood and gestured at their surroundings. Mr. B trotted to his dog bed in the corner, turned three circles and plopped into a contented heap.

The Wildes had grown up in the dance school. All of them—Tessa's cousins, as well as her siblings. Even her dog. Zander himself had taken classes as a kid. If he ever got married, his wedding waltz was sure to be one for the records. But considering he had *bachelor* written all over him, that wasn't likely to happen anytime soon. He lived in a hotel penthouse. Who did that?

"I have to teach. Mom needs the help," Tessa said.

"Maybe it's time for her to hire another teacher."

"She's not ready." Hiring someone new would mean

Tessa was leaving the school for good. Emily Wilde wasn't ready for that. For all Tessa's bravado, she wasn't sure she was ready for it either.

Opening night was in just two weeks. What if she wasn't ready? What if she failed spectacularly?

She was growing more accustomed to living in a world with sound again. It was making her a better dancer. She could feel the music now, flowing through her from head to toe. But the onslaught of noise still made her head spin. At the end of every day, she fell into bed and closed her eyes, grateful for a long stretch of silence.

"That's between the two of you, I suppose. But since you're spending so much time at rehearsal..." Zander shot her a grin. A grin of the charming variety, which meant he was about to bring up Julian again. "Perhaps you could speak to the elusive Mr. Shine on my behalf."

Bingo.

Tessa shook her head. "No."

"No?" Zander was so unfamiliar with the word that his eyebrows rose at least three notches.

"No," she repeated, tapping two fingertips against her thumb in the sign language translation for added emphasis.

Of all the things she might say to Julian, asking him to call her brother was nowhere on the list.

But Zander wasn't going to go down without a fight. "Why not?"

"For starters, I hardly know him." She swallowed.

It was blatantly untrue. The way he'd touched her proved otherwise. There was a *rightness* to the way his hands felt on her body…as if she'd been waiting for him all her life. Tessa knew how crazy that sounded. As much as she wanted to forget the pull she felt every time they were in the same room together, she couldn't.

Physical attraction aside, in the short time they'd been acquainted, Tessa felt like Julian knew her better than anyone else. Other than Dr. Spencer, he was the only one who knew that her hearing was beginning to come back, and she hadn't even had to tell him. He just knew.

He saw her, and despite his every effort to the contrary, she saw him, too.

And she knew him well enough to know that there was a reason he wasn't returning her brother's calls. "Julian doesn't want to play. I don't know what I could possibly say that would change that."

"I can think of a few things you could say." Zander's smile took on a decidedly sardonic quality.

Tessa's face went warm. "What's that supposed to mean?"

"It means that I've seen the way he looks at you. And I've seen the way you look at him. There's something going on between you two."

Something had *happened*. Past tense. And it had been a very big mistake. "You're imagining things."

"Deny it all you want, but the sparks flying between you and Julian Shine can be seen from outer space."

"I have the lead role in a ballet to prepare for. I've been fighting for this since I was a little girl. I can't afford a distraction right now. Besides, I just—" her throat grew thick "—can't."

"Look, I know what Owen said to you. He's an idiot. There's nothing broken about you, Tessa. There never has been. You're perfect just the way you are."

Just the way I am.

How am I?

She didn't know anymore. She wasn't part of the hearing world, yet she was no longer deaf either. She was somewhere in between. The strangeness of it left her feeling more lost, more broken than ever.

Even more broken than when Owen had called things off with her just four short weeks after her accident. They'd been dating for almost a year before she fell. Things had been serious. But after she lost her hearing, he hadn't lasted a month.

I don't feel connected to you. It's too hard to communicate. Maybe if the doctors thought they could fix you...

They'd been the most devastating words anyone had ever said to her. She'd wanted to scream.

I'm not broken. I'm still me.

But she'd choked on the words. She hadn't been able to get them out, probably because she'd been terrified they weren't true.

"Thanks, but I'm fine. Really." She forced her lips into a smile, even though she suddenly felt more like crying.

"Yes, you mentioned that," Zander said, making it clear he didn't believe her. "So, you'll talk to Julian?"

She rolled her eyes. "Nice try. I never agreed to do anything of the sort."

"Just invite him to Big Band Night. That's all I ask. Once he sees what a spectacular show we put on at

the Bennington, I think he'll be open to performing."
Zander Wilde, always the optimist. Especially when it
came to getting something he wanted.

Tessa wholeheartedly doubted he would in this instance. "You already invited Julian, and as I recall, he
declined."

"He might reconsider, seeing as it's tomorrow night."
Zander cleared his throat. "And you'll be there."

Of course she'd be there. Big Band Night was special.
It was her brother's baby and had made the Bennington
one of the hottest spots in New York again.

Tessa would be lying to herself if she tried to pretend
that the idea of seeing Julian outside the ballet studio
didn't send a forbidden thrill to parts of her body she'd
been determined to ignore since…

"You're wrong. I assure you," she said flatly.

"There's no harm in asking. Just do me this one
favor, and I promise I'll never mention his name to
you again. Deal?" Zander extended his hand, offering
to shake on it.

The dance-school door opened, and two of the students from Tessa's morning ballet class drifted inside,
along with a swirl of colorful fall leaves. She was running out of time to protest, plus her pumpkin latte was
growing cold.

Tessa sighed. She could always lie and tell Zander
she'd talked to Julian. He'd never know the truth.

Except he probably would. Knowing Zander, he'd
take one look at her and know she'd chickened out. He
had an annoying way of seeing right through her when
it came to matters of the heart.

I've seen the way you look at him. There's something going on between you two.

Her poker face needed work in a major way.

The door opened again, announcing the arrival of another student. Half the class was there now, peeling off coats and pulling on leg warmers and soft pink ballet slippers.

"Fine, I'll ask him," she blurted. *What am I doing?*

Zander grinned from ear to ear as she shook his hand. "Thanks, sis."

A series of images floated through Tessa's head. Images she forbade herself from paying any attention to whatsoever. Julian standing beneath the Bennington ballroom's belle epoque–style ceiling, with its tiny glittering stars shining on an indigo background. Julian taking her hand and leading her to the dance floor.

Julian's soulful blue eyes, fixated on her mouth as he said those words again. The words she still seemed to hear every time she closed her eyes.

Kiss me, Tessa.

"Don't hold your breath," she said. "The answer is going to be no."

It wasn't until after Zander left and Tessa was midway through barre with her adult beginner students that she wondered if she'd been issuing that sage piece of advice to her brother or to herself.

Julian paused at the threshold of the big rehearsal studio. Morning barre was set to begin in less than ten minutes. Most of the dancers were on the floor, bending themselves into impossible positions, readying themselves for class. A few of the ballerinas sat in a circle in the center of the room, sewing ribbons onto pointe shoes.

Tessa, however, was doing neither of those things. For some reason, she was perched on the piano bench. Waiting.

Julian's body went instantly into civil-war mode. His jaw clenched with resistance, but as usual, the sight of her threatened to bring him to his knees. They'd been tiptoeing around one another for the better part of a week. Julian had done his best to slip in and out of the building without ever allowing for a second alone with her.

He couldn't trust himself. That much was obvious.

But he couldn't just stand in the doorway all day. Besides, he wasn't likely to pin her against the wall and kiss her again in front of the entire ballet company.

Probably not, anyway.

He gritted his teeth and headed straight toward her. *This should be interesting.*

"Good morning." He dropped his messenger bag onto the floor and waited for her to get up.

She didn't. She stayed right where she was. Julian had no choice but to slide onto the piano bench beside her, where he was immediately enveloped by her scent—heady and floral, with a slightly fruity undertone. Like a bite of shiny red apple.

"Morning." She shot him a nervous smile.

Her hair was already swept into a tight ballerina bun.

Julian was so close to her that he could see the bobby pins holding her auburn waves in place. The memory of his hands in her hair hit him hard and fast…pins falling to the floor. Rich red tresses sliding through his fingers, as soft as silk.

He averted his gaze.

Tessa cleared her throat. "I need to ask you something."

"Are we ever going to talk about the fact that you can hear?" He glanced back up at her.

Her eyes grew wide. "Um…"

She glanced over Julian's shoulder, toward Ivanov and Daria conferring at the front of the room.

"I'm not going to tell anyone. But I'm definitely curious." He lifted a brow. "Can you blame me?"

She blinked. "Yes. I mean no… I mean, that's not what I wanted to talk to you about."

He narrowed his gaze. "Does anyone else know?"

"You're impossible. We're *not* talking about this right now." Her gaze flitted to his scar for the briefest of moments. "But to answer your question, no. No one else knows. Just you. Are you happy now?"

He was, actually. She'd overheard his secret, and he knew one about her. It seemed fitting. "What did you need to ask me?"

"I promised my brother I'd pass along his invitation to Big Band Night at the Bennington." Her gaze flitted to the sheet music on the piano, and then to the smooth wood floor. She seemed to be looking at anything and everything other than him. "He mentioned it to you last week."

Julian nodded. "I remember."

He remembered everything about that night, from the glittering sign that spelled out the name of The Circle Club to Tessa's buttercup-yellow dress. Perhaps most of all, he remembered the surge of relief that flowed through him when he learned that Zander was her brother and not her date.

Tessa stared at him for a beat and waited for him to say more. When he didn't, she nodded, and her bow-shaped lips curved into a smile that was too wide, too animated. "Right. I told him you wouldn't accept, obviously. But I promised I'd pass along the message, so…"

A knot formed in Julian's chest. *Don't say yes. Don't do it.* "If you'd rather I didn't go…"

Tessa shook her head. "That's not what I said."

"I see. So you'd like me to be there." He winked.

He was flirting with her now. Perfect.

He'd been right about trusting himself.

"I already told you that you're impossible, but it bears repeating." She laughed and gave his shoulder a little bump with hers. "You're impossible."

The knot in Julian's chest tightened, making it difficult to breathe.

He'd made her laugh. After everything he'd done wrong, she was sitting beside him. Laughing and flirting back.

He knew with absolute certainty that showing up at the Bennington was a bad idea. Having a conversation with her was one thing. Interacting with her family was another matter entirely.

Her brother would ask him to play the piano. Julian was rusty when it came to socializing, but he wasn't an idiot. Zander hadn't enlisted Tessa's help because he was interested in Julian's sparkling conversational skills. He was after a very specific thing.

Music.

Zander wanted the legendary Julian Shine to open his new jazz club. The poor bastard didn't seem to realize that that person no longer existed.

"All right, everyone. Take your positions at the barre. It's time for class to begin." Daria cast a purposeful glance at Tessa.

"I should go," Tessa said. But she remained seated beside him, with her slender thigh—barely visible through her pale pink tights—pressed alongside his.

He longed to touch her again. Really touch her.

Every time he came close to believing it could happen again, he remembered the look on her face when she'd heard Chance mention his burns. He didn't want to see that look again. If she ever saw him undress—if the dream of lying naked beside her, skin to skin, ever became a reality—he would.

Julian wouldn't be able to bear it. Not from her.

He wanted Tessa's kiss, her touch, her surrender. He wanted her light.

Not her pity.

"I'll do it," he heard himself say.

No. No, you won't.

But it was too late. Tessa was already beaming at him as if he'd hung the moon.

Julian could almost breathe again. "Tell Zander I'll be there."

Chapter Eleven

On the third Sunday of every month, the Palm Room at the Bennington Hotel changed from an ordinary, yet opulent, hotel ballroom into a glittering, 1940s-era wonderland. The transformation was staggering.

A bandstand was set up at the far end of the room, where musicians played tunes by Duke Ellington and Benny Goodman, while couples danced the night away beneath a massive crystal chandelier. Large round tables covered in swaths of ruby-red velvet ringed the perimeter of the ballroom. Each table boasted a centerpiece of plumed ostrich feathers and drapes of sparkling teardrop crystals.

It was really quite breathtaking. Tessa always half expected to see Humphrey Bogart and Ingrid Bergman out on the dance floor. Not tonight, though.

Tonight, she kept glancing at the ballroom entrance in hopes of seeing a certain cranky piano player. She couldn't even manage to sit still at the Wilde family table. Instead, she stood beside Zander near the bar, where he'd planted himself in anticipation of Julian's arrival.

"You're sure he said he was coming?" Zander plucked two glasses of champagne from a nearby tray and handed one of them to Tessa.

She rarely drank alcohol since she was usually preparing for an audition. She probably shouldn't indulge now either since opening night was just a week away. But she needed something to focus on besides Julian's absence.

Tessa took a tentative sip. The fizzy drink tickled her nose. "I'm absolutely sure. He's probably running late." *Or maybe he changed his mind.*

She highly suspected the latter. It was almost ten o'clock, and the band—a full jazz ensemble, complete with a rhythm section and a whole row of shiny gold trumpets, saxophones and trombones—was already into its second set.

He's not coming. She took a larger swallow of champagne. It was a nice, albeit somewhat dangerous, distraction.

What difference did it make whether Julian showed up or not? He'd only agreed in order to appease her in the moment and end their uncomfortable conversation. He'd probably never had any intention of actually coming at all.

How could she have been foolish enough to believe he'd actually show?

She'd even bought a new dress—a sleeveless, floor-length satin number with a beaded, cinched waist and wide padded shoulders. Daffodil yellow. When she'd spun through the revolving door of the Bennington and caught a glimpse of herself in the shimmering gold elevator doors, she'd felt like Rita Hayworth reincarnated. Now she just felt ridiculous.

This wasn't a date. It never had been.

She lifted her champagne saucer to take another sip, but the glass was empty. Tessa frowned. How had that happened?

"Thirsty?" Zander lifted a sardonic brow. "You're in rare form tonight, sis. If I didn't know better, I'd think you're looking forward to Mr. Shine's arrival more than I am."

"You couldn't be more wrong." She rolled her eyes, but her heart began to pound hard in her chest.

"Note taken." He seemed to be stifling a grin. "Would you like another glass of champagne?"

Absolutely not. "Yes, please."

Zander exchanged her empty glass for a full one.

She couldn't drink too much. She normally didn't indulge at all when she had a performance to think about.

Of course she normally didn't have an affair with the rehearsal pianist either.

She choked on a sip of bubbly. *It's* not *an affair.*

Far from it. If she were smart, she'd forget about him altogether. Julian obviously had some major issues.

Then again, so did she.

"Look who's finally here." Zander gestured toward the ballroom's entrance. "It's your boyfriend. I suppose that beautiful new gown you're wearing wasn't a waste after all."

If Tessa had been able to move, she would have punched her brother in the arm. Julian wasn't her *boyfriend*. She might be Zander's younger sister, but she wasn't a child. She was a woman. If anything, Julian was some strange combination of her lover and a total stranger.

And since when did Zander notice her clothes?

But Tessa couldn't punch Zander, because when her gaze landed on Julian, she froze. She was lucky she managed to maintain a grip on her champagne glass.

Julian stood beneath the gilded arch at the entrance to the ballroom, looking distinctly uncomfortable. At least Tessa thought it was Julian. Aside from his trademark glower, he resembled a completely different person.

He'd traded his customary dark, conservative suit for something on the opposite end of the fashion spectrum. He wore a slim-cut suit jacket, in a piercing navy blue. His necktie was just a slim strip of navy silk with a bright red heart in the middle, framed by a white zigzag design.

A *heart*. Tessa could hardly believe her eyes. Brooding, pensive Julian Shine was wearing a heart in the center of his chest. The heart was merely part of the pattern on his tie, but it was such an uncharacteristically hopeful symbol that she couldn't wrap her head around it.

She swallowed, and her hand started shaking. Champagne sloshed over the rim of the glass.

Tessa wasn't sure what to make of this new Julian. She blinked. Hard. Were those spectator wingtip shoes on his feet? Yes. Yes, they were. He looked like Don Draper, with a dash of Fred Astaire. Dapper. Charming. And just rakish enough to send a shiver of remembrance down Tessa's spine.

She stood still as stone while Julian's gaze swept the crowded ballroom. Her breath grew shallow. Every cell in her body tingled with awareness. Tessa had known for years that memories were every bit as physical as they were mental. Remembrance could live and breathe in flesh and bone.

Muscle memory, dancers called it.

Her body remembered his touch. It remembered the sensual brush of his fingertips and the sweet, wet warmth of his mouth. She could feel it now, as real as if he'd crossed the room and kissed her while he lifted the hem of her dress and trailed his hand up the inside of her thigh.

She shouldn't feel this aroused. She *definitely* shouldn't. He hadn't even made eye contact with her.

Zander waved and called Julian's name. He turned, gave Zander a curt nod and then locked eyes with Tessa as he approached.

She pressed her thighs together and took a generous gulp of champagne. Her head spun a little. Damn Zander and his plentiful trays of Dom Pérignon.

"Mr. Shine, so glad you could make it." Zander beamed and shook Julian's hand.

"Good to see you again." Julian nodded. His gaze slid to Tessa and back to Zander again.

Tessa's stomach did a little flip, and when Julian bent to kiss her cheek in greeting, she realized why.

It felt like a date. She still knew it wasn't, but it felt like one, all the same.

He hadn't even brought Chance. Just himself.

Tessa took a deep breath while Zander launched into an explanation of Big Band Night—what it was and the reasons he'd originally thought it would be a good fit for the Bennington. He'd wanted to honor the hotel's rich history with Lawrence Welk and Guy Lombardo, both of whom had performed at hotels like the Bennington, in a way that would bring a glamorous ambiance back to the building. It had been a phenomenal success. So phenomenal that once a month, Zander's hotel was one of the hottest spots in Manhattan.

Julian nodded and actually smiled a few times during Zander's monologue. He seemed genuinely impressed. But his gaze kept darting back to Tessa, and she felt the heat in his sapphire eyes down to her toes.

"I want to take Big Band Night a step further and really cater to the jazz crowd. Real jazz, with altered chords, modal harmonies, progressions…that kind of thing," Zander said.

Julian gave him a crisp nod. "Free jazz."

"Exactly." Zander grinned.

Tessa knew precisely where he was headed. So did Julian, if the sudden stiffness in his posture was any indication.

Sure enough, Zander went in for the kill. "That's what The Circle Club is all about."

He was going to offer Julian a job. A job that Julian didn't want to discuss in any way, shape or form.

Tessa wanted to strangle Zander all of a sudden. The night had been lovely so far. She didn't want it to end with an awkward job offer that would remind Julian of all that he'd lost.

She had to stop what was happening.

Zander's smile widened. "I think you'd be a great fit…"

"Dance with me." Tessa grabbed Julian's hand.

His fingers, warm and strong, closed over hers. Her head swam with images of his hands flying over black-and-white keys, making music. Piano hands.

Zander cast her a hard glance. "We're in the middle of a conversation."

"Not anymore." Heart hammering, she thrust her empty glass at him and then leaned closer to Julian, as if he was her partner and they were about to dance a *pas de deux*.

Except it wasn't at all like that. She never felt this breathless, this electric when she was about to dance with Chance. Or anyone else. "Let's go."

Julian's gaze fixed unwaveringly on Tessa's supple spine as she led him by the hand to the dance floor. The ballroom could have been crumbling down around him in a pile of gold leaf and crimson velvet, and he'd have never noticed. Her dress draped into a low dip right at the small of her back, and the sight of her porcelain back mesmerized him. So lithe, so graceful. He was transfixed.

And more than a little tempted.

He shouldn't be there. He shouldn't be sliding his arm around Tessa into a dance hold, with her supple, bare back against his fingertips. He shouldn't be pulling her so close against him that he could feel the heat of her body through the diaphanous fabric of her satin dress.

Yet here you are.

"I'm sorry about my brother." Tessa peered up at him through the thick fringe of her lashes.

Something deep inside Julian shifted, as if clicking into place. God, how much champagne had he consumed?

He cleared his throat. "It's fine."

She rolled her eyes. "It's not. Please tell me you have relatives who annoy you sometimes, too."

Julian stared at her for a beat. He didn't want to talk about his family. Not now. He just wanted to dance with her. A part of him had probably been waiting to dance with her since the moment he'd first seen her gliding across the ballet-studio floor.

But the last time he'd shut down on her, she'd fled. With good reason. So he exhaled a tense breath and shifted his gaze someplace else. Anywhere other than her sympathetic emerald eyes. "I don't have much family. My mother died when I was nineteen. My father left when I was a kid. He resurfaced briefly, but after my accident, he pulled a disappearing act again."

After my accident…

It was the first time he'd mentioned the car crash to Tessa…or to anyone, for as long as he could remember.

The words felt rusty coming out of his mouth. But there they were, hanging in the air like dark clouds.

"No brothers or sisters?" Tessa asked softly.

"No, but Chance is like a brother. We've known each other since we were kids. And he certainly qualifies as annoying at times."

Tessa's eyes glittered. He drew her closer as the music changed. "Did you just make a joke, Mr. Crankypants?"

He was tempted to make another one, possibly about turning her over his knee and spanking her if she kept calling him that. But he refrained. "I'm not all bad."

Her lips curved into a coy smile. "I know you're not."

Julian was suddenly overly aware of the hotel key card tucked into the front pocket of his suit jacket. The concierge had handed it to him when he first arrived.

Compliments of Mr. Wilde.

Zander was courting him. Pulling out all the stops. Julian was certain that Tessa's brother hadn't paused to consider that Tessa herself might end up in that room… in his bed.

Julian hadn't considered it either, because it wasn't going to happen.

But the way Tessa was looking at him right then made the key card impossible to ignore. It was like a stick of dynamite in his pocket.

"You and Zander seem close," he said, by way of distraction.

Still, the concierge's words as he'd slid the key across the marble counter, toward Julian, echoed in his consciousness.

The Duke Ellington Suite, sir. Featuring floor-to-

ceiling windows, sweeping views of Central Park and a baby grand piano.

"We're close." Tessa nodded. The copper highlights in her hair shimmered beneath the ballroom's crystal chandelier. "I had an accident a while back, too. I fell."

"I know," he said, his voice raw and rusty again.

It would have been dishonest to pretend they lived in a vacuum. She hadn't acted as if she'd been unaware of his past. He owed her the same.

"Zander has been very protective of me since then. My whole family has. Sometimes it gets a little…"

"Stifling?" Julian lifted a brow.

"Exactly, which is why I haven't told them I can hear." She bit her lip, and Julian made a Herculean effort not to look at her mouth. He failed miserably. "I can sort of hear, anyway."

"Sort of. What does that mean?"

"I can only hear out of my right ear, not my left. It just started happening a little over a week ago. During auditions."

That explained her astonished expression and the freedom in her dancing. Julian remembered thinking that Tessa's body moved as if she'd never heard music before. It had been truer than he'd realized.

"Your family would probably be thrilled if they knew." They seemed like the real deal, unlike Julian's father, who'd only turned up in Julian's life once he'd gotten his first gold record.

Still, Julian had wanted to believe his father was back to stay. Right about the time he'd convinced himself it might be true, Julian had climbed into a car with

Chance after the Grammy Awards. His career was gone overnight, and so was his father.

"My hearing isn't like it was before. Everything's so loud. Distorted. It might not even last. My doctor advised me to stay home for a month or so to try and get used to it."

He was beginning to understand. "But if you did that, you'd have to give up your part in the ballet."

"Precisely. I can't do that. I won't. My mom...even Zander...would insist on it if they knew. They care, and I love them for it. Sometimes they just care a little too much. I've been waiting a long time for something wonderful to happen. And now it is. I don't want to wait anymore."

They weren't just talking about ballet anymore.

The flicker of heat in Tessa's gaze gave her away. She was thinking about the night they'd almost spent together. He was thinking about it, too. Every touch, every taste, every sigh. Julian remembered them all. He couldn't look at her anymore without longing to re-capture what had happened in that empty ballet studio. Night and day, he wanted her.

More than wanted...he *ached* for her.

"I have to live my life." Tessa's voice dropped to nothing more than a hoarse whisper. Her gaze dropped slowly, sensually, to Julian's mouth.

He went instantly hard.

If her family hadn't been watching from just a few feet away, he would have kissed her again, then and there. They were swaying to the sounds of another era, in a ballroom that had witnessed generations of life's celebrations and sorrows. Maybe it was the magic of their surroundings, or maybe it was the fact that Julian was dressed in a suit he'd once worn onstage, but he felt himself being pulled into the past. Back to a time when he wouldn't have hesitated to take Tessa to bed, to lay her down on the crisp white sheets that waited upstairs and bury himself inside her until the sun came up over Central Park.

I have to live my life...

How long had it been since Julian lived? *Really* lived? Chance would have had the answer at the ready. He'd been harping on it for months now, and he was right. Julian hadn't lived since the night of his accident. Shutting himself up in his apartment wasn't a life. He'd been existing, not living.

For a while, it had been enough.

It wasn't anymore.

He knew that now. Deep down, in a place that Julian seldom allowed himself to acknowledge, he'd probably known it all along. But the night he'd kissed Tessa— the night he'd watched her come so blissfully apart— had changed things. For a few breathless moments in a darkened dance studio, he'd lived.

If he could get that moment back, he might have done things differently. He might have let her see him. All of him. He might have focused on her and her alone, instead of the mirrors that had surrounded them on every side. He might have given into the unrelenting desire to be inside her, scars be damned.

Turning back the clock wasn't possible, though. Julian knew that better than anyone. But Tessa's parted lips and the look in her eyes said otherwise. That look slayed him, and it had a name…

Bedroom eyes.

He needed to leave…now, before he did something they'd both regret. The mirrors had stopped him before, but they weren't at the ballet anymore. They were in a luxury hotel, full of fizzy champagne and music that made him feel like something other than what he was. It was like a fever dream, vivid and lush.

The song they'd been dancing to wound to a close, and the band's horn section launched into a brash intro of something new. Julian recognized the tune before the lyrics started. They were playing "Dance, Ballerina, Dance" a somewhat obscure song, performed first by Vaughn Monroe and later by some of jazz's greatest. Nat King Cole's version had always been Julian's favorite.

He swallowed hard. *Ballerina.* Why did it seem like the universe was trying to tell him something?

The lead vocalist crooned, "Dance, ballerina, dance…"

Tessa's eyes grew wide, and her cherry-red lips curved into a giddy grin. "What is this song?"

Julian pulled her closer, so that her body was flush against his, and then dipped his head so his lips grazed her ear. "Careful, you're not supposed to be able to hear, remember? You're giving yourself away."

He pressed a chaste, tender kiss to the spot just below her earlobe. It was meant to be a diversion, just a way to hide the fact that he was talking to her. But it didn't stop there, because somehow that simple brush of his lips felt like the beginning of something. A prelude, a promise.

Before he realized what he was doing, Julian's mouth

slid lower to kiss the gentle curve of Tessa's neck. It was a real kiss this time, decadent and openmouthed. His lips lingered long enough for him to feel the flutter of her pulse and the shiver that coursed through her willowy body.

Julian pulled back to look at her. Her cheeks were flushed, and her eyes had gone deliciously dark. She seemed more than a little unsteady on her feet all of a sudden. Shaken. Weak in the knees.

The song played on. "Whirl, ballerina, whirl…"

"Let's leave. Let's go somewhere, just you and me. I want to be alone with you again," she whispered. "Please, Julian."

They'd come to a complete stop on the dance floor. Couples spun around them, twirling to the music, and Julian was scarcely aware of any of them. It was all just a blur. Tessa was all he could see, and the impossible things she was asking of him were all he could hear. All he *wanted* to hear.

He looked at her long and hard. "You don't know what you're saying."

She was offering herself to him, offering him her balletic body and aching grace. He wanted her to be certain. He needed her to promise him that if they went down this road, she wouldn't change her mind once he undressed and she saw his marred body, his ruined flesh.

But he couldn't demand such a promise. He knew that.

He also knew that if he didn't take her to bed, the ache of wanting her might kill him.

"I know exactly what I'm saying. I'm saying I want to see you. I want to touch you, and I want you inside me. Now...tonight." She was shaking like a leaf, but her gaze was unwavering.

What must it have taken for her to say those words to him after he'd denied her before? Julian couldn't imagine. He didn't deserve this. He didn't deserve *her*. And he couldn't deny her again if he'd tried. He knew it, and so did she.

"Tessa." His voice broke, and something deep inside him seemed to break along with it.

She placed the palm of her hand against his chest, directly over the red heart on his tie. "I want you, Julian. As you are right now, the man standing in front of me."

Without another word, she took his hand again. This time, she led him away from the glittering ballroom. Away from the happy chatter, the swaying couples and starlit ceiling.

To a place where they could truly dance.

Live, ballerina, live.

Chapter Twelve

A knot of panic gathered in the pit of Tessa's stomach. She'd never acted this way before. With anyone. She'd never, ever looked a man in the eye and told him she wanted him. Most certainly, never a man who'd rejected her in the past.

As frightening as it was, there was something empowering about coming right out and saying it aloud. It was as intoxicating as it was frightening. The words had bubbled up her throat. There'd been no stopping them.

I want to see you. I want to touch you, and I want you inside me. Now...tonight.

There wasn't an inch of her flesh that Julian hadn't seen. Touched. Kissed. But Tessa had never felt so naked, so vulnerable, as when she uttered those words.

She'd been holding on to them for a while now—resisting her desire for him, trying to tamp it down. But once she told him how she felt, her whole body seemed to exhale. It was a relief to let go, to fully live in the moment, rather than worrying about what might happen a day from now…a week, a month. Tessa knew better than anyone how unpredictable the future could be.

Whatever happened between her and Julian next would change things. Tessa couldn't begin to think what it would be like to see him at the studio after tonight, but she didn't care. Not now. Sometimes change could be a good thing, couldn't it? Even when that change was altogether unexpected.

After her fall thirteen months ago, Tessa had been convinced her life was over. Everything she'd wanted—everything she'd dreamed about and worked so hard for—no longer seemed possible.

She'd been wrong, though. She hadn't lost ballet. It meant more to her now than ever before.

She was tired of trying not to fall again, both literally and metaphorically. The constant effort it took to keep herself protected at all times was exhausting. She couldn't do it anymore. Maybe tomorrow she'd feel differently. Maybe Julian would change his mind once more and walk away, leaving her feeling humiliated two times over.

Tessa couldn't think about that now. Just once, she wanted to fling herself toward what she wanted with wild abandon.

Right now, what she wanted was *him*.

Fingers entwined with his, she held her head high and strode out of the ballroom. Zander, deep in conversation with a group of people at one of tables closest to the dance floor, didn't seem to notice. Good. No doubt he'd pepper her with questions later, but right now he was one less thing standing in her way. If they stopped to chat with her brother, Julian might rethink things. If he did, she'd never have the courage to proposition him again.

Since Owen, there hadn't been anyone else. Tessa hadn't been on a single date in over a year, much less in a man's bed. She'd believed the hurtful things Owen had said to her. They'd cut her to the quick, probably because as harsh as he'd seemed, there was an undeniable truth to the fact that she felt isolated sometimes.

She couldn't keep up with conversations. Being around people was stressful. She was always struggling to understand what was being said. It was easier not to try.

She'd plunged deeper and deeper into silence. Even when Owen had been sitting right beside her, she'd felt so lonely sometimes that she couldn't breathe.

Once he'd broken things off, Tessa no longer believed it was possible for a man—or anyone—to really know her. Maybe it wasn't...but for the first time, she wanted to believe. She'd wanted to believe since the moment Julian first looked at her. She'd felt that midnight-sapphire gaze down to her core, as real as a caress. That phantom touch had been her undoing.

Now she stepped out of the noisy ballroom and into the hush of the gleaming marble lobby, with Julian alongside her. Silence wrapped itself around them. Tessa felt many things in that moment, but loneliness wasn't one of them. She was hyperaware of her pulse pounding in her ears and the tiny rays of silver light the overhead chandelier cast on the smooth tile floor. It almost looked like stars were falling all around them.

She turned toward Julian, half expecting him to order her to go back to the ballroom without him. *Not that. Please, not that.*

"Shall we ring for your car?" she asked. There was a waver in her voice, a slight tremor of breathless anticipation.

Julian tightened his grip on her hand. "No need. I have a room."

Then he was suddenly the one leading her, instead of the other way around. He strode purposefully across the lobby, and she walked alongside him, with the sweeping hem of her yellow gown trailing behind her.

She felt like a princess. She felt beautiful. *Wanted.* And when they stepped into the elevator and the doors slid shut, closing them inside, she felt wanted even more.

Julian's mouth was on hers before they lifted an inch off the ground. Maybe she was dreaming, or maybe she was just fooling herself into believing something that wasn't real, but this kiss felt different than the others. It felt like more than a kiss, somehow. It felt like an aching, overdue apology.

And yet the moment his fingers wound through her hair, tipping her head back so he could deepen the kiss, Tessa was instantly reminded of how good he could make her feel. Warm. Delicious. Liquid. Like she had honey flowing through her veins.

She sighed against his lips, and he groaned, pressing into her so her back was pinned against the mirrored elevator wall. The shock of cold on her bare back caused her to arch into him even more, and he dipped his head to kiss the hollow of her throat.

Her knees buckled. If she hadn't been braced against the wall, she would have dissolved into a puddle at his feet. She could feel Julian's erection pressed against her center, just as she had earlier on the dance floor. Only he seemed even harder now. Impossibly hard.

And big. Far bigger than she'd anticipated.

Maybe he'd been right…maybe she didn't know what she was asking for. Tessa could handle the scars. Julian had seen her at her most vulnerable. She was ready to see the real him, flaws and all. His scars were a part of him, a part he'd kept hidden for far too long. Tessa wanted to be the one who unraveled his mystery. She wanted to touch him and kiss him—*everywhere*—and make him feel as beautiful as she felt when he looked at her.

But she was beginning to realize that she wasn't at all prepared for the intensity of sex with Julian. They hadn't even made it out of the elevator, and she was already flooded with want and need. So much so that it scared her a little.

Julian didn't touch her the way that Owen had. Owen had barely touched her at all. He'd seen her as a fragile waif, too easily broken to be properly kissed.

Not Julian.

She should have known it would feel this way, so tortuously overwhelming. It had been this way before, back in the ballet studio. She still couldn't think about that encounter without her face going hot and flushed. She marveled at the way she'd behaved that night. It had been so unexpected that sometimes Tessa thought it had been nothing but a sublime dream, a wishful fantasy. But then she'd remember the way the night had ended and the pained regret in Julian's gaze after she'd come apart, and she'd known it had been real. That kind of humiliation couldn't be imagined.

This time will be different.

It would. There would be no regret this time. No unfulfilled needs. She wouldn't lie in bed alone afterward, with tears running down her face, wondering how he could have left her spent and breathless and then just walked away.

This time, they would finish what they'd started.

Julian planted his palms against the mirrored wall on either side of her head, hemming her in. He was much taller than she was, and as a result, her gaze was dead even with the solid wall of his chest. She stared at his tie—at that bright red heart—and for some reason, her throat grew thick.

Because this means something. He means something.

Julian's mouth dropped to her breast, and his teeth caught her nipple through the fabric of her gown. Tessa released a shuddering gasp, and her eyes drifted shut.

Too fast. Too stimulating. Too *much.*

What was happening? Were they even going to make it to the bedroom?

The elevator bell chimed, and her eyes flew open.

She found Julian regarding her with fire in his gaze. He looked as though he was on the verge of picking her up, carrying her to his suite and tossing her onto the bed. The idea that he might do that very thing sent a wave of divine heat straight to her core.

"Are you sure about this, Tessa?" His jaw clenched.

Wordlessly, she reached between them and stroked his hard length through the barrier of his trousers.

She was sure.

Julian let out a sound somewhere between a moan and a growl. It was a primitive, animalistic noise, and he was certain he'd never heard anything like it come out of his mouth before.

What had come over him? He was on the verge of taking her, right there...in the elevator of her brother's hotel.

"Not here," he whispered through clenched teeth, catching her wrist with his hand. He needed her to stop. Now, before he let the elevator doors close again so he could bury himself inside her as quickly as possible.

She nodded, wide-eyed, and licked her lips. It took every ounce of restraint he could muster to prop the elevator open and wait for her to glide past him into the hallway. He said a silent prayer of gratitude when he saw a nameplate with elegant black script on the door closest to them.

The Duke Ellington Suite.

"Here we are," he murmured.

Either he didn't say it loud enough or he'd forgotten which ear Tessa could hear out of, because she didn't react. She kept walking, and for a second or two, Julian let her so he could watch her beautiful, bare back in motion without worrying about being reprimanded for ogling.

He never tired of watching her move. Whether she was dancing or simply walking from one end of a room to another, she moved with a feline grace that left him reeling.

Julian had loved music since he'd been old enough to know what it was. He didn't just listen to a song…he experienced it. When he heard Miles Davis, he could feel a slow burn deep in his marrow. Clifford Brown accompanying Sarah Vaughan on the album they recorded together just a year before Brown's death, at just twenty-five, was so full of devastating promise that it made Julian weep. For as long as he could remember, music had made him *feel*. It still did…even after all this time.

Watching Tessa just then, he realized something. Seeing her move drew something out in him. Every time. When she danced, he felt it deep in his chest. It moved him. Whether it was a stunning arabesque or something as simple as a slow turn of her wrist during an adagio piece, Julian felt her movements as if she were a song.

His song.

He swallowed. She wasn't his. She never would be. He wasn't altogether certain he'd be able to go through with making love to her tonight, much less anything beyond that.

She'll change her mind soon enough.

Julian was convinced she would. But he didn't want to think about that right now. He couldn't. He'd moved beyond the ability to be rational about whatever was going on between them.

"We're here, babe," he said, louder this time. He caught up with her and slid his fingertips down the inside of her forearm, capturing her hand in his.

When she stopped, he kissed the back of her hand, and she flashed him a coy smile.

He placed his hand on the small of her back and led her back to the suite. Their eyes met and held as he slipped the key card into the lock. The moment the door opened, they crashed into one another and tumbled into the room midkiss.

More.

His blood roared in his ears. He needed more of her. So much more. He needed everything.

He scooped her into his arms and carried her to the bed, sidestepping the grand piano in the center of the room. The lights of the city shimmered all around them through the suite's floor-to-ceiling windows. They were on top of the world. Alone. Just as Tessa had wanted.

She reached for the top button of his shirt, and Julian's hands clenched into fists. The urge to take her hand and stop her was so strong, it made his head ache. He had to fight it with every cell in his body.

You want this.

He did. He wanted *her*. He wanted to lose himself inside her beautiful body. He wanted to make her come apart again. For just a night, he wanted to forget the ugliness of the past and present, to forget the man he saw every day in the mirror and remember what it felt like to be part of something bigger than himself. To connect with someone.

He *needed* her.

He needed her as surely as he needed to take his next breath.

Desire, longing and need were all woven together in a tightly bound knot in Julian's gut. He'd been doing his best to ignore the knot, to keep it tied firmly in place, but he couldn't do it anymore. It had been unraveling for days now. When Tessa stroked him in the elevator, the knot had come loose. All the feelings he'd been denying were unfurling, coursing through him, refusing to be ignored for a moment longer.

He groaned.

Tessa moved from the top button to the second one and then quickly to the third. Her hands shook, but she never broke her gaze. Not once. Julian needed her to be certain, and she was. Her eyes glittered with it, telling him without a doubt that the tremble in her fingertips was a product of anticipation, rather than nerves.

She paused after the third button, spread the collar of his shirt open wide and kissed his exposed skin. It was a gentle kiss at first. Tender. Reverent. But just as Julian's fists began to unclench, Tessa's lips parted, and the kiss turned into something far more sensual.

Her tongue explored his small patch of exposed chest as she moved to straddle him on the bed. The folds of her yellow gown billowed around him, and suddenly his erection was aimed right at her center with nothing but the thin layer of his trousers between them. She was light and heat, and Julian was drowning in her warmth, more aroused than he thought possible. He groaned and reached for her hips through the sea of yellow satin. With his hands clasped just below her waist, he ground his erection more firmly against her, while her mouth moved lower—nuzzling, licking, exploring.

It was like being kissed by sunshine. He was half out of his mind, on the verge of coming, before he realized that Tessa's fingers had started moving again, deftly unbuttoning the rest of his shirt.

Somewhere in the back of his head, alarm bells were going off. He ordered his hands to release their hold on her, to stop her before she ran her fingertips over the scar tissue that covered the left side of his rib cage and extended all the way down his hip. But his hands flagrantly disobeyed and instead reached around, splayed on her bare back, and then dipped lower to slip inside the waistband of her gown and cup her bottom.

He'd lost control—of the situation, of his body, of his mind—and he didn't give a damn. It felt good to let down his guard. *Dangerously* good. He barely flinched when Tessa peeled his shirt away. Her mouth was on his, and she'd begun to grind against him, and he was so turned on, so eager to dispense with their clothing and make love to her that he nearly forgot he hadn't allowed anyone to touch him in two years.

"Is this okay?" Tessa whispered, her breath hot against his ear as she placed a hand on his scarred flesh.

At first, he felt almost nothing, which was to be expected. His nerve endings had nearly been burned away. On the surface, he was damaged beyond repair. But beneath the outer layer, he still had sensation. She began to caress him, and he could suddenly feel her touch deep down. It was a shock to his system.

A shudder racked his frame.

But was it okay? Yes.

Julian nodded. He attributed his refusal to speak to concerns about whether or not she'd hear him, but on some level, he knew the truth was far more complicated. He didn't quite trust himself to answer her question aloud.

He wasn't sure if the acute sensitivity he was experiencing was an actual physical response, or whether it was all in his head. He just knew that if he tried to speak, his voice might break because something profound was happening to him. Being touched again was unleashing a torrent of emotion. He was feeling everything at once, from pain to pleasure, lust to love.

No, he thought. *Not love.*

He wasn't in love with Tessa. They barely knew one another. He was just reacting to being touched after months of self-imposed isolation. His body was being flooded with hormones signaling attachment and intimacy. It wasn't love. It was biology.

"Lie back," Tessa whispered, and then she pushed on his chest until he was reclining against the pillows.

Julian exhaled a ragged breath. His head was spinning. He couldn't think. He couldn't seem to do anything but feel. Tessa sat astride him, gazing down at his chest, and he felt it as keenly as he would a caress.

She was seeing the worst of him. Raised, red flesh that resembled candlewax more than skin. Uneven ridges that he knew felt unnaturally smooth and slick beneath her fingertips. The first time Julian had seen his torso after the bandages were removed, he'd retched. Granted, he'd healed since then. He'd also grown accustomed to the sight of his scars now, but he knew they looked bad. Bad enough that the only women who'd seen his bare body in the past two years had been medical professionals, who'd taken in the sight of him with either clinical indifference or, worse, sympathy.

He saw neither of those things in Tessa's eyes as she lowered her head and kissed his damaged flesh. He saw only want and need and desire…the same things he was feeling, mirrored back at him in the emerald depths of her gaze.

"Don't the scars bother you?" he asked before he could stop himself.

"Honestly?"

"Yes, tell me the truth." His throat tightened.

He didn't want the truth. Not tonight. Not if it would hurt.

"They don't bother me at all. They're a part of you, just like your eyes, your feet, your hands." She wove her fingers through his. "Have I ever told you how much I love your hands? I love the music you make with them. I love the way you use them to speak to me. I love the way they feel on my body."

He cupped her breasts and ran the pads of his thumbs over her nipples, through the wisp-thin fabric of her gown. "Tell me what else you love."

Love.

That word again.

Julian swallowed with great difficulty.

"I love your body, Julian. All of it." She bent to kiss him. First on the mouth, and then lower—his neck, his shoulder, his chest. Her mouth traveled over every inch of burned skin—slowly, *worshipfully*—while her hands went to work on his belt buckle.

Julian released a tortured hiss.

He wasn't sure he believed her. He didn't know if what he felt right now was real, or if she was telling him a beautiful lie. It didn't matter. If she was lying, so be it. He'd hold on to the illusion until morning. While moonlight spilled through the windows and Manhattan's glittering skyline glowed and twinkled all around them, he'd let himself believe. He'd believe she still wanted him as much as he wanted her. He'd believe he was the kind of man she deserved.

He'd believe it enough to make her scream his name while he was buried deep inside her.

Tessa unzipped his fly, freeing him, as she continued kissing her way down his body. Then, before he could brace himself, she took him inside her mouth, and he had to close his eyes because the sight of her, bathed in starlight and pleasuring him, was just too much to take.

"Tessa," he groaned, reaching for her, burying his hands in her hair.

It was too much. It felt too damn good. He wasn't going to last if she didn't stop. But he was slipping under, letting himself fall to a place where there were no lies, no truths, no painful memories to overcome. There was just pleasure and grace and the coppery softness of Tessa's hair sliding through his fingers…the exquisite warmth of her mouth. He wanted to stay there as long as he could. Forever would have been nice.

He opened his eyes. "Babe, I need you to stop."

She released him, peering up through the thick fringe of her eyelashes. Her gown slipped off one shoulder, and Julian didn't dare move. He didn't breathe. If he did, he'd climax then and there. He was mesmerized by the sight of her—the pristine shoulder, elegant collarbone, lips, cherry red and bee-stung from pleasuring him.

Forever.

The word rang in his head like a song from his past.

Tessa reached behind her to unzip her dress, and it fell into a silky pool of yellow on the bed. In one swift move, Julian rose up onto his elbows and switched their positions, so she was under him. Finally, he was in control.

That's what he told himself, anyway, as he slipped a finger inside her and bent to take a perfect, rosy nipple into his mouth. But there was nothing controlled about the arousal pulsing through his veins when she arched beneath him. He'd barely touched her and already she was pulsing against his hand, ready to come apart. Ready...for him.

He positioned himself at her entrance, and she reached for him, guiding him home. With a single thrust, he entered her. Somewhere in the distance, Julian thought he heard music—a song so lush, so lovely, he nearly wept. He knew it couldn't be real. It was an illusion, just like so much about this night.

But then Tessa rose up to take him fully inside—

every part of him, scars and all—and the rhythm wrapped itself around his heart. Soulful. Pure.

Achingly sweet.

Chapter Thirteen

Sometime during the night, Tessa woke up and realized she was alone in the bed.

Eyes closed, her body pleasantly languid and tender, she stretched like a cat and reached for Julian. But the spot beside her was empty, and the sheets were cold to the touch.

He's gone.

She couldn't believe it. He'd *left*. After everything they'd done, he'd sneaked away in the middle of the night. A cold trickle of unease snaked its way up her spine.

She sat up and clutched the sheet to her bare body, squinting into the darkness. Moonlight streamed through the suite's floor-to-ceiling windows, casting a faint light on the strange surroundings, and she realized she wasn't alone after all. Julian was sitting at the spectacular grand piano, situated in the center of the room.

She gathered the sheet around her and walked toward him with fine white fabric trailing behind her as if it were the train on a dress. Her throat closed when she realized he'd put his shirt back on. But he'd left it unbuttoned, and he was still naked from the waist down. That was something.

"Hi," she said.

He looked up, and his features relaxed into an easy smile—the kind of smile she never thought she'd see on Julian Shine's face. The tightness in her throat loosened a bit.

Everything is fine.

Of course it was. Things were more than fine. He'd let her see him. She'd touched him. She'd kissed him. They'd made love. There was no reason at all for the nagging sense of dread that she couldn't seem to shake.

Julian hadn't gone anywhere. He was right there, with his hands dancing over the piano keys. Smiling.

"Sorry if I woke you," he said. "There's a melody in my head. I want to get it down before it slips away."

Tessa swallowed. "It's okay. You didn't wake me."

He reached a hand toward her. "Come here, beautiful."

Her stomach did a little flip as she drew closer. He swiveled on the piano bench to face her and wove his fingers through hers to reel her in for a kiss that left her more than a little unsteady on her feet.

He took her face in his hands and looked her directly in the eye. "It's my turn now. Let me see you."

Her skin broke into a riot of goose bumps, but she

did as he asked and dropped the sheet. Julian was already fully aroused, as if he'd been biding his time, waiting for her to wake up so he could ravish her once more. The thought brought a rush of heavenly warmth to her center.

She wanted him again. Tender, sweet and excruciatingly slow this time. She wanted it to last.

And last.

With the tip of his pointer finger, Julian traced the shape of a heart on her belly. Tessa's head spun, as if she'd done a whole series of dizzying pirouettes. She'd wanted passion. She'd wanted to feel swept away again, like she had that night in the dance studio, when he'd left her a shivering, quaking mess of need. He'd given her those things again tonight. He'd given her everything she'd wanted.

But this...

This tenderness was more than she'd expected. It left her feeling raw and vulnerable in a whole new way, like she was trying as hard as she could to grasp something that was forever out of reach.

"Julian," she pleaded.

He kissed her breasts and ran his hands down the back of her thighs, pulling her into his lap to straddle him. Then his hands slid to cup her bottom, and she lowered herself onto his erection with a shuddering gasp.

How could it feel so good again? So right? Would it be like this every time?

She closed her eyes and arched her back, reveling in the way he filled her. It was exquisite. *He* was exquisite, in every way.

The burn scars didn't bother her. She'd been telling him the truth when she'd said they were simply a part of him, just like any other part.

He was at odds with his own body. The same body that made such beautiful music had also betrayed him. He still heard songs in his head, but he could no longer play the trumpet. The man he saw in the mirror now was a partial stranger.

Tessa knew what it was like to live like that. She'd experienced her own bodily civil war, embracing the graceful stretch of her limbs and the turnout of her feet, while also wishing she could be someone else from the neck up. She used to wish very hard for her love of dance to just wither and die. It would have made the past year so much easier. She hadn't felt whole since the day she'd fallen, and she knew Julian felt that way, too.

Maybe now things would be different.

For both of them.

This wouldn't be the last time they made love. There would be more nights like this. There had to be. She needed this as much as he did.

She slid her hands into his hair, anchoring herself to him as his thrusts grew deeper. She clenched around him, drawing a deep moan of pure male satisfaction from his lips as she went liquid inside. The pressure gathered and built, bearing down on her with an intensity that nearly made her weep.

And yet, somewhere beneath the swirl of desire, something was wrong. Very wrong. Tessa could sense it, but she was too lost in the delicious heat of the moment to figure out what it was. Her climax tore through her, and she cried out Julian's name with tears streaming down her face.

It wasn't until he reached to brush them away that she realized what was so terribly wrong.

His hands. Julian's lovely, musical hands had been moving up and down the piano keys when she'd first found him sitting at the piano. He'd been playing a song.

But Tessa hadn't heard a single note.

Dr. Spencer didn't mince words. It was a quality that Tessa usually appreciated, but in this instance, she would have preferred a little sugarcoating. "I'm afraid the news isn't good, Tessa."

Mr. B trembled in Tessa's lap. She ran a soothing hand over the little dog's head and blinked backed tears.

She couldn't cry. Not now. The early-morning emergency appointment with her doctor would already make her late for rehearsal. Walking into the studio red faced, with tears in her eyes, in front of the entire company would only make things worse. Not to mention the fact that if she cried, she wouldn't be able to read Dr. Spencer's lips. Sadly, that was once again a major necessity.

She took a steadying inhale. *No tears.* "I don't understand. For weeks now, I've been able to hear. It was strange at first, but I've been getting used to it. I've been *relying* on it."

Dr. Spencer's gaze narrowed. "Relying on it? How so?"

"For dance." Tessa swallowed. A lecture was surely coming her way.

"You've been dancing? I was under the impression

you've been staying at home, avoiding unnecessary stimuli as I recommended."

Tessa's face went hot. She'd been doing the exact opposite, of course. Other than a quick stop at the brownstone this morning to change out of her evening gown and pick up Mr. B, she hadn't been home at all for the past sixteen hours. Prior to that, her life for the past few weeks had been an endless cycle of not enough sleep, followed by teaching class and heading straight to rehearsal. There'd also been the extra practice sessions in the evening, not to mention the significant detour into Julian's bed at the Bennington.

The phrase *unnecessary stimuli* echoed loudly in her consciousness.

No.

She refused to think about it that way. The night before had been very, very necessary. If she hadn't been so blindsided by the fact that she couldn't seem to hear anymore, she'd still be in bed with Julian right then. Instead, she'd rushed away as soon as the sun came up, citing her morning class at the Wilde School of Dance as an excuse, even though adult ballet never met on Monday morning.

She could have told him the truth, of course. But she didn't want to. The night they'd spend together had been magical, and Tessa wanted to keep it that way. At least that was the excuse she told herself. On some level, she knew the reason was far more devastating.

She was afraid. Tessa was terrified to her core.

Admitting to Julian that she suddenly couldn't hear would have made it real, and that couldn't be the case.

She wanted to hear him play the piano again. She wanted to hear her name falling from his lips and the low growling sound he made sometimes when he kissed her. She wanted to keep dancing to actual music. There had to be some sort of explanation, some way to fix whatever had gone wrong.

But apparently there wasn't, because now Dr. Spencer was sitting across a desk from Tessa, telling her the news wasn't good.

"Remember the audition I told you about? I got it. I was cast as the lead and made a full member of the company. I couldn't walk away from that." Should she have walked away? Would it have made a difference?

"Congratulations." Dr. Spencer nodded, but she looked less than thrilled. "So you've been rehearsing all this time? You haven't given yourself any chance to adjust to the changes you've been experiencing?"

Tessa fought the urge to argue, because in essence, the doctor was correct. "There hasn't been time. The show opens this weekend."

Four days from now.

If she could no longer hear the music, she'd have to relearn her part all over again, using different cues. It would take weeks of practice. Not days. She was going to lose her part. She'd probably even lose her place in the company. It would be as if the past few weeks had never happened at all.

"Tessa, the last time you were here, you were distressed. You told me you didn't want to hear." The sympathy in Dr. Spencer's gaze was too much to bear.

Tessa wanted to scream. *Can't you just fix this? Fix*

me? *Please.* But she'd been asking those questions for over a year. Some things were impossible to fix. She should have understood that by now. "I changed my mind."

Her mind wasn't the only thing that had changed. *Everything* had changed. She hadn't realized it at the time, but the moment her hearing returned, her whole life had turned itself around. She was a real ballerina now. She had Julian. She'd even begun to think she might be falling in love...

And now she was supposed to go back to how things were before?

Dr. Spencer balled her right hand into a fist, placed it against her chest and moved it in a clockwise motion. She was signing. *I'm sorry.*

Tessa heart nearly cracked in two.

She'd come full circle. She was back to silence and signing and struggling to keep up with simple conversation. Back to being the dancer who couldn't hear and would never keep up. Back to reading lips.

Before long, she'd be right back to feeling lonely again.

She hugged Mr. B tighter to her chest. "Could it come back?"

"Anything is possible. Like I told you during our last appointment, head trauma is unpredictable. Your hearing test this morning indicates profound loss in both ears, just as it did before. The past few weeks could have just been an aberration. Or they could have been an indication of things to come. Right now, the only thing we can do is wait. Time will tell."

Tessa sat very still and nodded. On the inside, she

was screaming in protest. Time was the one thing she didn't have.

"Very well, then. Drop by if anything changes. My door is always open." Dr. Spencer stood, signaling the end of the appointment.

Tessa shook her hand, attached Mr. B's leash to his collar and followed the little dog outside. A gust of wind sent her hair tumbling from its ballerina bun. The air was thick with the scent of roasting chestnuts and spiced apple cider. She felt cold all over, as if winter was nipping too closely on fall's heels.

As she made her way through the city streets, which were bustling with sounds she could no longer hear—taxi drivers honking their horns, sirens wailing, the rumble of the subway underfoot, the music of Manhattan—Tessa began to cry.

This time, there was no stopping the flow of tears. She went ahead and let them fall.

Much to Julian's dismay, he found Zander Wilde waiting for him in the hotel lobby, on his way out of the Bennington.

He would have much preferred a different Wilde sibling, specifically the one who'd slunk away from his bed in the early hours of the morning. Tessa had grown pensive as the sun came up. Quiet. While she got dressed, he'd sat on the piano bench—where they'd made love just hours before—and played "Dance, Ballerina, Dance" for her and gotten no reaction whatsoever.

He was trying his damnedest not to read too much into her suddenly bashful behavior. She'd given him no concrete reason to believe her feelings for him—assuming she had any—had changed. As he understood it, she had a ballet class to teach before rehearsal. It meant they couldn't spend a lazy morning with breakfast in bed and more lovemaking, as he'd envisioned, but it was fine. She had responsibilities. They both did. The world hadn't stopped spinning simply because he'd taken her to bed.

Still, something felt off. He wished it didn't. He wished so hard that, by the time Zander approached him in the lobby, his jaw hurt from clenching his teeth so hard.

"Mr. Shine, I hope you enjoyed your stay." Zander gave him a wide, easy smile that could only mean he had no idea that his sister had spent the night with Julian in the Duke Ellington Suite.

Julian wasn't about to fill him in. "It was a pleasure."

"Excellent. Do you have a minute to chat before you run off?" Zander glanced at the gold clock hanging from the gilded crown molding.

The time was just shy of 8:00 a.m. Julian didn't need to be at the studio until 10:00 a.m., which Zander was probably well aware of. He and Tessa were close. He was part of the family that prided itself on keeping a watchful eye over her. Julian wouldn't have been surprised if Zander knew his sister's schedule like the back of his hand.

Julian had no choice but to agree to Zander's request. "Sure."

"Wonderful. Step right this way, and I'll have some coffee brought round." He escorted Julian to a pair of deep green velvet chairs, in a sitting area off the side of the lobby bar. The sign for The Circle Club loomed large, which came as no surprise. "Would you like anything in particular?"

"An espresso, please. A double." He should have asked for a triple. He hadn't exactly done much sleeping in the magnificent suite, and now he was going to have to fight off Zander's request to play the piano at his club, when all he really wanted to do was make sure Tessa wasn't mired in regret about giving herself to him.

His gut churned. It wasn't true. There hadn't been a trace of hesitancy in her gaze when she'd unbuttoned his shirt and seen his scars for the first time. She'd accepted him. She'd *loved* him. The things she'd said to him still echoed in his consciousness. He heard them every time he closed his eyes.

I love your body, Julian. All of it.

Zander slid a bottle of San Pellegrino and a demi-tasse cup, brimming with dark espresso, onto the small table, situated between the two chairs. Julian took a sizable swallow of the sparkling water and then sipped his coffee, while Zander launched into another passionate description of his plans for his new jazz club.

To his credit, he sounded like a true jazz aficionado. He'd not only done his homework, but he'd invested a huge amount of money into the place. Original vinyl recordings by greats like Hank Mobley, Tubby Hayes and Rosemary Squires were framed and hanging on the walls. He'd also somehow acquired the piano that Thelonious Monk had played at Carnegie Hall, on one of his rare appearances during the 1970s.

"Impressive." Julian placed the demitasse cup back on its saucer.

"Would you like to play something on it?" Zander nodded toward The Circle Club's closed door.

Hell, yes, he wanted to play the Mad Monk's piano. But not if it meant making a promise he knew he wouldn't keep. "Sorry to disappoint you, Zander. I appreciate the offer, but I don't play much jazz anymore."

If he agreed to headline The Circle Club, the news would be splashed all over New York City. Zander would make certain of it. Once word got out, every music critic in the tristate area would turn up to see the great Julian Shine onstage again.

Except Julian wasn't great anymore. He wasn't nearly as good on the piano as he'd been on the trumpet. He was painfully aware of that fact. He sure as hell didn't need to read about it in the *New York Times*.

Zander nodded. "Tessa told me you'd say that."

At the sound of Tessa's name, Julian's libido went on high alert. He slung back the remainder of his espresso.

"She's rather fond of you, you know," Zander said, lifting a brow. "That doesn't come easy for her, especially after all she's been through."

"Her fall. Yes, I know about that." Julian gave a curt nod. He wasn't altogether comfortable with the direction the conversation was headed. It felt wrong to discuss Tessa behind her back.

"It wasn't just the fall. It's everything that happened afterward. Losing her hearing was devastating. Then Owen left, just when she needed someone most."

Owen? The name sounded vaguely familiar. "Her dance partner?"

"He was her dance partner." Zander sighed. "And more. He blamed himself for her hearing loss. If you ask me, it's because he knew her injury was his fault to begin with. He couldn't handle the guilt of what he'd done. That makes him a prick in my book, but it left Tessa feeling broken. She doesn't think she's worthy of a real life. Real happiness."

Julian's gut churned. He had the sudden urge to find the despicable-sounding Owen, wherever he was, and pummel him within an inch of his life.

He'd dropped her. Then he'd walked away.

No wonder she had trust issues.

"Tessa's special," Julian said, as a heaviness hit him square in the center of his chest. "I have no intention of hurting her. I promise you that."

"Good." Zander nodded and glanced at the clock again. "I thought she might join us. She usually drops by on Monday mornings, before rehearsal, but she must have something else going on today."

The heavy sensation in Julian's chest intensified. He felt like a vise was closing around his heart. He cleared his throat. "I thought she had to teach a ballet class this morning. I seem to recall her mentioning something about it last night."

This morning, actually.

And she'd most definitely mentioned it. Julian remembered the conversation with perfect clarity— since they'd both been naked at the time.

Zander shook his head. "The studio is closed on Mondays. Always has been. I ought to know. My entire life as a kid was centered around the operating hours of the Wilde School of Dance."

"Of course." Julian gave him a grim smile. The darkness was gathering inside him again. Suffocating and black as night. "My mistake."

Tessa had lied her way out of his bed this morning.

He needed to get out of there. He couldn't keep sitting in the Bennington, pretending to have a normal conversation with her brother, while his mind was spinning with a million possibilities, each one more humiliating than the next. Tessa wasn't the only one with trust issues.

She'd lied to him.

Why?

There had to be an explanation. He couldn't have misread her reaction the night before. She'd been so ready...so *responsive*. He hadn't imagined the way she shivered every time he looked at her, how she writhed when he touched her. She'd climaxed the instant he'd pushed inside her velvety heat. He could practically still feel her pulsing around him. She couldn't fake that kind of passion. No one could.

"I should be going." Julian stood. He needed answers, and he wasn't going to find them here. "Thank you again for your hospitality."

Zander shook his hand. "Anytime. Think things over, and if you change your mind about The Circle Club, give me call. I promise to make it worth your while."

Change his mind?
Not likely.
Not anymore.

Chapter Fourteen

Chance leaned against the rehearsal studio piano and drummed his fingers in an obvious attempt to get Julian to look up.

Julian shook his head and kept playing his warm-up scales. He wasn't in the mood for a discussion. Not with Chance, anyway. He wasn't even sure he wanted to talk to Tessa. At least not here. He just wanted to bang out some music on the piano, earn his paycheck and then get out as quickly as possible.

But in true Chance form, Julian's oldest friend wasn't willing to be ignored.

"I know you see me standing here, man." He waved a hand directly in front of Julian's face, much like he used to do when they were kids and he grew bored of Julian playing his trumpet all the time.

Julian sighed and looked up. His hands kept traveling over the keys. D chord, E flat, F, G. "What do you want?"

"Your girlfriend is missing," Chance said.

The piano went silent. Julian didn't bother correcting him this time. *She's not my girlfriend.* "What are you talking about?"

"Tessa's not here. She was supposed to arrive an hour ago for a costume fitting, and she never showed. Ivanov is on a terror. That tutu is covered in half a million dollars' worth of diamonds. I thought you might have some idea where she could be." The Russian's voice boomed from the direction of the hallway. Chance rolled his eyes. "Please say you do, or else we're in for a long, painful day."

Shit. Where was she?

"I don't." Julian raked a hand through his hair. Something was wrong. Very wrong.

"Great." Chance rolled his eyes. "When was the last time you saw her?"

Julian met his gaze, but said nothing.

Chance's brow furrowed. "What aren't you telling me?"

Julian wasn't keen on discussing what had transpired between him and Tessa. Aside from the obvious fact that it was private, he also wasn't entirely sure what, if anything, was going on between them, thanks to his chat with Zander.

But he was also beginning to worry. It wasn't like Tessa to forget a costume fitting. Especially this one. Tessa hadn't even been a minute late to rehearsal since the second day of auditions, when she'd crashed into him. "I saw her earlier this morning."

Chance lifted a brow. "Interesting. Does this mean what I think it means?"

Good question. Julian wished he knew the answer. "It means I'm concerned as to her whereabouts. Nothing more. Has anyone tried to reach her?"

"She has a cell phone, but she only texts because of the you know..." Chance gestured to his ear. "I sent her a message earlier but haven't gotten a reply."

Dread settled in Julian's gut like a lead weight. He pulled his cell phone out of his pocket, along with the business card Zander Wilde had pressed into his palm before he'd left the Bennington. He didn't want to call Tessa's brother. He didn't even want Zander Wilde's number in his phone, but desperate times called for desperate measures.

Zander picked up on the first ring. "Julian! It's great to hear from you so soon. I hope this means you've reconsidered my offer."

"I'm sorry, but no. Actually, I was wondering..." Before he could finish, he looked up and saw Tessa darting into the room. Her face was flushed and streaked with tears, and Mr. B was tucked under her arm. But she headed straight to her usual spot at the barre, pulled her pointe shoes out of her bag and began the complicated process of putting them on while her little dog sat and watched.

Julian's jaw clenched. He didn't bother telling himself that Tessa wasn't his and whatever was going on with her wasn't any of his business. They'd spent one night together. He didn't have any kind of claim on her.

But that night meant something. It wasn't just sex.

It meant something because he *cared*. As much as he'd tried not to, he did. He might even be in love with her.

"Julian, are you still there?" Zander's voice echoed in his ear.

"Apologies. I seem to have misdialed." He hung up without waiting for a response, stood and marched toward Tessa.

Chance muttered something behind him, which he ignored. He couldn't sit on a piano bench and play scales when Tessa was so visibly upset.

She'd been crying.If he'd had any part of whatever was making her so upset, he'd never forgive himself.

One of the other dancers reached her before he did. Violet, if he remembered correctly. She was huddled beside Tessa, peppering her with questions, when he slowed to a stop directly in front of them.

"Tessa," he said.

She didn't respond. Not even a flicker of acknowledgment. Julian felt like he'd stepped back in time, to the day he'd first tried to talk to her on the train. A rush of coldness came over him, reaching icy fingers straight to his core. He thought about the song he'd played for her just hours ago—"Dance, Ballerina, Dance"—and the disappointment that nagged at him when she hadn't remembered its significance. He cursed himself.

She doesn't hear me.

How had he missed the signs again?

Mr. B pawed at Tessa, prompting her to look up. She took in his presence and smiled. But even as her generous lips turned up at the edges, her eyes filled with tears. "Hello, Julian."

Violet shot him a curious glance.

"We need to talk," he said, wishing with every fiber of his being that he could offer her some kind of comfort. The urge to pull her into an embrace and hold her was so strong that he had to cross his arms to stop himself from doing so.

Violet looked him up and down. "She can't. She already missed a costume fitting, and rehearsal is about to start."

"I think Tessa can speak for herself." Julian's gaze flitted from Violet's annoyed countenance back to Tessa. "Can we talk?"

He placed his right hand against his heart and moved it in a deliberate, clockwise circle. *Please.*

Tessa nodded. "Yes, but not here. Meet me in my dressing room."

Violet grabbed her wrist. "What are you doing? Have you seen Ivanov yet? He's on the warpath."

She gathered Mr. B in her arms and stood. "He can wait. I'll be right back."

Violet stared at her in disbelief and then gave Julian a look that was dripping with disdain. Apparently he was ruining her career now. Perfect.

He followed Tessa out the door and down the hall, toward the dressing rooms. Mr. B peered over her shoulder, with his ears pricked forward and bright eyes trained on Julian. The dog seemed to like him. That was something.

"Where is she? Is she here yet?" Ivanov yelled from behind a nearby closed door.

Julian was tempted to swing the door open and put

him in his place. It was a wonder he hadn't strangled the guy by now.

"Here." Tessa stopped at the door marked Principal Ballerina and motioned for him to enter. "Come on in."

Julian stepped inside and closed the door firmly behind him. The room was tinier than he'd imagined, only large enough to contain a small, sagging sofa and a tiny desk, with a matching chair. A mirror, surrounded by vanity lights, hung above the desk. The only other thing on the wall was a poster of a dancer, whom he recognized from his childhood. Big eyes, willowy limbs. She looked a lot like Tessa, minus the glittering fire in Tessa's eyes and the winsome quality of her movements, along with the way he seemed to hear music whenever he was in her presence.

He swallowed. Hard.

Tessa deposited Mr. B on the sofa and turned to face him. He wanted to touch her. Not doing so was killing him. The only thing stopping him from kissing her right there and then was the unshed tears shimmering in her emerald eyes.

"When?" he said. And despite his determination to be strong for her, to be someone she could rely on, his voice broke.

"I'm not sure what you're asking me." She tried to smile, but the slight quiver in her chin didn't escape his notice. "When what?"

"You don't have to pretend with me. I know you can't hear, Tessa." Did she think it mattered? He didn't give a damn how they communicated, so long as they actually did. "When? What happened?"

She gave him a watery smile and shrugged one slender shoulder. "The doctor doesn't know why. She warned me it might not last, and she was right. I'm not entirely sure when it went away. Sometime during the night. When I woke up and found you playing the piano, I knew something was wrong, but I couldn't put my finger on it. I'd just slipped back into silence so easily, so naturally, that I didn't notice at first. And now..." She pressed her fingertips to her lips and shook her head.

Julian's chest felt like it was being ripped wide-open while he waited for her to finish.

She took a deep breath. "And now everything's changed. It's over."

"Nothing's changed, Tessa. You're still the same person you were last night." Pain blossomed in Julian's temples, like some kind of terrible flower.

He was the biggest hypocrite in the world.

Chance had said various versions of the same sentiment to him on countless occasions, and Julian railed against it each and every time. Now here he was, looking Tessa in the eye and telling her what was happening to her body didn't matter.

But it didn't. He believed that with every shred of his being.

"I'm not the same person, Julian. Yesterday, I was a dancer preparing for the opening night of her first big role. Today, I'm once again a wannabe ballerina who can't hear. Don't you see what's happening? I'm going to have to quit."

He couldn't have been more stunned if he'd been slapped in the face. "What are you talking about? No one at the company knew your hearing was coming back to begin with. They don't care about that. Not even Ivanov. It doesn't matter."

"It matters, Julian. It matters a lot. The only reason I got this part is because I could hear again. Now it's gone. I'll never be able to keep up. Maybe if I had more time…but I don't. Opening night is in four days." She took a deep breath. An eerie calm had come over her. It scared Julian to death, because he knew what it signified.

Defeat.

"You can't quit," he said flatly. He wouldn't let her. If she dropped out of this ballet, there wouldn't be another. She could do this. If she didn't believe in herself enough to do it now, she never would.

"It's my decision, not yours." Her cheeks flared pink.

She was angry. Good. Julian preferred anger to despair any day of the week. He'd gladly step in as the object of her rage if it meant she'd cut herself some slack.

"You're right. It's not my decision, but I can't stand by and watch you make a mistake you'll regret later." *Tell her, damn it.* "I care about you, Tessa."

For a fraction of a second, there was a crack in her composure—just a sliver of a moment when Julian caught a glimpse of the woman who'd taken him by the hand the night before and led him out of the ballroom. Her gaze locked with his, and he could tell by the look in her eyes that she was remembering every decadent minute of their time in that hotel room. Every kiss, every shudder, every sigh.

He reached to cup her face, and a shock of something pure and primal shot through him.

Love.

He was in love with her. He'd never been so sure of anything in his life.

Tessa cleared her throat and took a backward step. The room was so small that she was still barely an arm's length away, but it felt like a mile. "I appreciate that, but…"

Julian filled in the blank for her. "But you don't believe me."

Her gaze shifted to the floor. "Rehearsal is starting. I should go. I need to talk to Ivanov and Madame Daria."

It was now or never. If he let her walk away, he might not have another chance to tell her how he felt, to make her believe him. He stood very still and waited for her to shift her gaze toward him again before he spoke.

It was the longest minute of Julian's life.

Look at me, damn it.

Finally, when he couldn't wait anymore, he reached for her again. He took her chin in his hand and gently forced her to look at him so she could read his lips. "I understand what you're going through, babe. Believe me, I do. It's unfair that you have to go through it twice, but this time, you don't have to go through it alone. I promise."

Her bottom lip quivered, and she inhaled a ragged breath. She looked like a frightened animal.

In his gentlest voice, Julian said, "Marry me."

Tessa's eyes flew open wide. *"What?"*

Mr. B jumped to attention on the sofa and let out a

bark. Marvelous. Even her dog found the idea of marriage too shocking to contemplate.

Julian got it, though. He'd shocked himself, as well. But the instant the words left his mouth, a feeling he hadn't experienced for a long time fell over him like a shimmering, sublime curtain.

Peace.

He'd been troubled and restless for so many months that he almost didn't recognize it. He wouldn't have now, if Tessa hadn't opened his eyes. She'd taken him inside her heart and body, and his world had fallen back into place. And now he wanted her to stay there with him. Forever.

"Julian, you don't want to marry me." Tessa shook her head. "Have you lost your mind?"

He arched a brow. "I think I've found it, actually."

She blinked. "This isn't a joke."

"I know. I'm not laughing. I'm dead serious." He took her hand in his and ran the pad of his thumb over her ring finger, right at the spot where an engagement ring would sit.

She stared at their interlocked hands for a beat, and her gaze softened. Then she looked up again. "If you're actually serious, I have two questions for you."

"Shoot."

"Did my brother talk to you again this morning about playing at The Circle Club?"

Julian frowned. It was the last thing he expected her to say, and for the life of him, he didn't know what relevance The Circle Club had to the matter at hand. "Yes, he did."

Tessa stared at him for an overlong moment. Julian had a sinking feeling he knew what her next question would be. "And did you accept his offer?"

"You know I didn't."

She dropped his hand. It was a test, and he'd clearly failed.

"You're not going to marry me because I won't play at your brother's jazz club?" he asked, incredulous.

"No. I'm not going to marry you because nothing has changed. How can you believe in me when you don't even believe in yourself?"

Julian didn't have an answer for that, probably because she had a valid point.

He let out a long, tense exhale. "Don't do this, Tessa. If you don't want to marry me, fine. I'm a big boy. I can take it. Just don't quit the ballet. Don't give up."

One of them had to have the courage to live. She'd proven her point—it wasn't him. It had never been him, never would be. But since day one, he'd always believed in Tessa. He couldn't stand by and watch her give up. He knew where this road would lead, probably because he'd walked the same path himself.

"Promise me," he said through gritted teeth.

"I can't," she whispered.

So he did the only thing that made sense. He turned and walked out the door. Mr. B hopped off the sofa and pawed at his legs, but Julian kept on walking. He walked past the rehearsal studio and kept going for the full length of the hallway until he found himself standing outside, where there were no more ballerinas. No

Ivanov or Madame Daria. No stacks of sheet music waiting for him on the piano in the corner.

If Tessa was willing to quit, then so was he.

Chapter Fifteen

It took Tessa three full days to wrap her mind around the fact that Julian wasn't coming back to the ballet.

She'd been so shaken by their conversation that she'd walked into the rehearsal studio and stood silently, mind reeling, while Ivanov berated her for missing her costume fitting. Of course that had been after she'd been forced to go running after Mr. B, who'd tried to follow Julian wherever he'd gone.

She couldn't believe what had happened. Julian had asked her to *marry* him. Even more surprising, she'd nearly said yes. She'd had to clamp her mouth closed to stop the word from flying right out of her mouth.

She'd done the right thing, of course. He couldn't possibly want to marry her. Not really. Not when her life was in complete and total disarray.

He made it sound so easy, though. All of it...even the ballet. But what did he know? He wanted her to risk making a fool out of herself when he wouldn't even entertain doing the same.

Still, she never imagined he'd walk away. She'd believed him when he said she wouldn't have to go it alone anymore. She hadn't realized quite how much she believed him until he'd disappeared.

Because you pushed him away. Face it.

"Are you ready for dress rehearsal tonight, darling?" Emily Wilde's rapidly moving hands as she signed caught Tessa's attention.

She had a feeling it wasn't the first time her mother had asked the question. Tessa was sitting opposite her at the breakfast table, but her mind was elsewhere. As it had been a lot lately.

"Honestly, mom, no. I'm not." She put down her fork. She didn't feel like eating. Nor did she feel like dancing. The only reason she'd stuck it out this long was because every time Ivanov flailed his arms at her for being off beat, every time she made a mistake, every time she started to say the words "I quit," she saw the look in Julian's eyes when he'd begged her to keep going.

Don't give up. Promise me.

Even after she'd turned down his marriage proposal, and after she'd so cruelly thrown his refusal to return to jazz in his face, he'd believed in her.

Just like he'd sworn he would.

Tessa's mother frowned. "Not ready? But you've been working so hard."

"The truth is I'm not sure I can do it. I've been having some issues with my hearing. Sometimes I think it would be better if I stepped down and let the Cast B lead take my place." Tessa released a breath she hadn't realized she'd been holding. She sat back and waited for her mother to agree with her. Right after she interrogated Tessa about her hearing issues.

But her mother's response caught her decidedly off guard. "That's ludicrous," Emily signed.

Tessa blinked, not quite sure she'd properly understood. "I thought you'd agree with me."

"Why on earth would you think that? For weeks now, I've watched you practice night and day. You've given this role everything you've got. You've earned this, darling."

Tessa's gaze narrowed. Who was this person, and what had she done with Tessa's mother? "Aren't you going to ask me about the hearing problems I mentioned?"

Her mother took a sip of coffee and gently placed her mug back down on the table. "I don't need to ask. You've been experiencing intermittent recovery."

"You talked to Dr. Spencer?" Tessa couldn't believe it. Wasn't there such a thing as doctor-patient confidentiality?

"No. You're an adult, darling. Dr. Spencer wouldn't discuss your case with me if I begged. I know that because I might have tried that once or twice." She shrugged.

If Tessa hadn't felt so much like crying, she would have laughed. This was the Emily Wilde she knew and loved. "Then how did you know?"

"Because you're my daughter. I've known you since

before you were born. I saw the signs. That's why I've been so concerned about you. I thought it might be best if you stayed closer to home."

Tessa blinked back a fresh wave of tears. "I thought you made all those comments about teaching full-time because you didn't think I could handle the part."

Her mother reached for her hand and gave it a squeeze. "I believe you can do anything, darling. The show opens tomorrow night. You can't quit now. Not when you've come this far. How are your ears? Are you experiencing any dizziness that could affect your balance?"

"No. It's nothing like that. For a while, I could hear, though. At first it was really disorienting, but then…" She swallowed around the lump in her throat. *Then it was wonderful.* "Then it went away."

Tears glistened in her mother's eyes. "I'm so sorry."

"I'm okay." To Tessa's astonishment, she almost believed it.

"Hello? Anybody home?" The front door of the brownstone slammed shut, and Zander walked into the kitchen, swiveling his gaze back and forth between the two women. "What's going on in here? Am I interrupting some kind of mother-daughter crying jag?"

"We're fine." Emily gave Tessa's hand another squeeze. "Aren't we, darling?"

Tessa nodded. "Yeah, I suppose we are."

For the most part, anyway. There was still the matter of her broken heart, but that was a lost cause. Surely Julian despised her now. His absence spoke volumes.

"What do you need, Zander? Doesn't that fancy hotel of yours still serve breakfast?" Emily lifted a brow.

"I came to pick up my tickets for Tessa's performance tomorrow night. It's going to be a busy night at the Bennington, so I'm afraid I'll have to meet you both at the Lincoln Center. I'll probably be running late."

Emily stood. "Zander Wilde, you'd better not miss your sister's big night."

He held up his hands in surrender. "I'm not. I promise I'll be there. Can I have my tickets, please?"

"I'll go fetch it." Their mother gave him a playful swat on her way out of the room, but he ducked and her hand narrowly missed his handsome head.

"Who are you bringing as your date tomorrow night?" Tessa asked.

Zander shrugged. "No one special." It was the story of his dating life. He never kept a girlfriend long enough for Tessa to remember her name.

Zander shot her a curious glance. "Speaking of dates, have you spoken with Julian lately?"

Tessa's heart stopped at the sound of his name being dropped so casually in her family kitchen. She cleared her throat. "Not lately." *Not since he asked me to marry him and I turned him down flat.*

"Perhaps you should," Zander said.

"What's that supposed to mean?" Tessa gathered her plate and coffee cup and headed for the sink. She needed to get to the studio in time to warm up before dress rehearsal. Also, she wasn't at all ready for a casual conversation about Julian. She probably would never be ready for that. It hurt too much to say his name. It hurt to think about him.

Unfortunately, not thinking about him had proved to be impossible.

Zander followed her and spun her around so she could read his lips. "It means that maybe you should check in with him and see what he's up to."

"I can't. Julian doesn't want to have anything to do with me." Not that she blamed him. Hot shame coursed through her at the memory of how she'd responded to his proposal.

She knew how difficult it was for him to open up. She'd worked hard to break down his defenses. And the moment he'd let himself be vulnerable, *truly* vulnerable, she'd shut down.

She'd accused him of not believing in himself, even as she'd been on the verge of walking away from the most important role of her career. God, could she have been a bigger fraud?

Zander shook his head. "I doubt that's true."

"You don't understand." Julian might not have believed in himself, but he'd believed in her. More important, he'd believed in *them* when Tessa couldn't. "It's over."

The text came just as Julian was about to take the stage. If his phone hadn't been tucked into the inside pocket of his suit jacket and set to vibrate, he would have missed it. He wouldn't have seen Tessa's message until it was too late.

Opening night. I just want you to know that you're the reason I'm dancing tonight. I know I have no right to ask you this, but please come.

He stared at the words on the screen as the other musicians, already onstage, started in on the intro. The band was a classic jazz trio—a double bassist, a drummer and Julian on piano. The grouping had been Zander's idea, and Julian had to admit it was pretty genius.

He'd called Zander the day after the terrible discussion with Tessa in her dressing room. Not because he was trying to win her back, but because she'd been right.

He'd been in no position to tell her what to do. She'd had a moment of weakness. She'd been terrified of failing at the one thing that meant the most to her, and he'd walked right out the door. The way he'd behaved was no better than what Owen had done to her, or what Julian's father had done to him after his accident. Every time he thought about that awful day, he hated himself a little bit more. He should have stayed. He'd just proposed marriage to her and promised to stick by her side, but the minute she'd spoken the truth about what a coward he was, he'd turned his back on her.

All this time, he'd been telling himself he couldn't play jazz because it wouldn't be the same. He'd never be as great as he once was. But he'd never even tried. What difference did it make, anyway, if he loved it? Wasn't that what he'd told Tessa when she'd said she was dancing for herself, not for Ivanov?

He should be playing music for himself. Not the music critics. Not the press. Not Madame Daria. He should play because his life had become meaningless without it. And if he failed, so be it. At least he'd given it all he had.

Predictably, Zander had been thrilled to hear from him. He'd also been full of ideas about how to make Julian's debut as painless as possible, starting with the trio. He wouldn't be alone onstage. He'd have support. Years ago, Julian would've balked at the suggestion. He'd been great on his own. Now, he knew better. There was no shame in needing help. Tessa had taught him that.

Now here he was, about to perform for the first time since his accident. He was on the verge of conquering his demons or, at the very least, taking a good swipe at them. And suddenly, the only place he wanted to be was sitting in a red velvet seat at the Lincoln Center, watching Tessa dance.

It's too late.

He looked past the stage, out into the crowd. The Circle Club was packed from wall to wall. If he bailed now, he'd make a fool out of Zander. He couldn't do it. Zander was Tessa's brother. He'd staked his reputation on tonight. He'd even agreed to Julian's request to open the club on the same night as the opening of the ballet. He'd needed the distraction. Otherwise, he would have shown up just to see if she'd go through with it, or if she'd quit.

She hadn't, though. She was dancing tonight, and now Julian wouldn't be there to see it.

The intro was nearing its conclusion, and his bandmates were already casting him worried glances. Zander was probably sitting at one of the tables near the front row, white as a sheet. Julian needed to get onstage.

He typed out a return text and pressed Send as quickly as he could.

I can't. I'm sorry.

Then he slipped his phone back into his pocket and strode toward the piano. The club swelled with applause before he even sat down. This was what he'd been dreading most—the moment when the room held its breath, expecting something great. Something perfect. Julian imagined himself crumbling beneath the weight of the cheers.

It wasn't like that at all, though. He felt buoyed by ovation, shot clean through with adrenaline. His hands shook slightly when he placed them on the keys, so he took a deep breath and counted to three. Then he launched into the song he'd chosen for his comeback. "Dance, Ballerina, Dance."

The music seemed to flow straight from his soul, out to the tips of his fingers. He made it through the verse, and then the chorus. When he launched into the verse again, the cheers of the crowd grew so loud that he could barely hear the sound coming from the instruments. The rest of the song passed by in a blur of whirling, twirling chords, punctuated by extended bits of improvisation. Jazz at its most pure.

When it ended, Zander walked onstage amid the ear-splitting applause to shake Julian's hand before the next arrangement. He said something, but Julian couldn't make it out above all the noise.

"What?" he asked, and then he realized that Zander had pressed something into his palm during their hand-shake.

He looked down and saw that he was holding a front-row ticket for the ballet.

Zander moved closer so Julian could hear him. "I said get out of here. You can play a full set tomorrow night. Unless there's no place else you'd rather be right now?"

Julian's fist closed around the ticket. "Thank you."

Zander shrugged. "Anytime. Just go before you're too late."

Lincoln Center was a fifteen-minute drive from the Bennington on a good day of the week, but the streets were teeming with traffic. Julian took the hotel limo, at Zander's insistence, but by the time the ballet was scheduled to start, the car hadn't even made it to Central Park.

He wasn't going to make it. Tessa's solo was in the first half of the program, as was her *pas de deux* with Chance, including the dreaded angel lift.

"Pull over," he said.

The driver met his gaze in the rearview mirror. "But, sir, we've still got quite a way to go."

"It's fine. I'll walk the rest of the way."

Julian didn't walk.

He ran.

He ran as if his life depended on it, and he got to his seat just as Tessa glided onstage. At some point during the performance, he was vaguely aware of Zander slipping into the chair beside him. Tessa's mother and sister were seated farther down the aisle. At least he thought they were. Julian couldn't focus on anything or anyone but Tessa.

She was magnificent.

He sat in the darkened theater long after the performance ended. Through the standing ovation, all three curtain calls. And even as the people around him gathered in the aisles and headed toward the grand lobby, with its shimmering crystal chandelier, Julian remained in his red velvet chair. Motionless.

He couldn't seem to make himself get up. Or even move. Had he clapped when the performance ended and the curtain swished closed? Had he yelled "Brava" as Tessa lowered into a deep curtsy at center stage, or had it been the man behind him? He didn't even know. He'd slipped into some sort of trance.

God, she'd been exquisite.

Julian had known she could dance. He'd seen the way the music moved through her body with tremulous, aching grace. Even before he'd known her. Before he'd loved her. He'd recognized her talent back on that very first day. Before he'd known about the silence.

Before...

But tonight she'd danced like something out of a dream. He'd never seen anything so beautiful in his life. Not even close.

Perhaps it was best that he'd let her go. He didn't deserve a woman like Tessa. He never had, and now was no different. Tonight was supposed to be a new beginning. For them both. She'd reached out to him, and he'd screwed that up, too. He'd told her he couldn't come watch her dance.

Did she know he'd been there? He should have never sent that text message. *I can't. I'm sorry.*

Regret fell over him like a dark velvet curtain. Then a loud noise from the right of the stage caught his attention—the sound of a door slamming shut.

His head jerked in the direction of the clamor, and his heart stopped.

Tessa.

She'd come for him.

She ran down the aisle, still dressed in ruby-red tulle and sparkling diamonds, with a dazzling tiara pinned in her upswept hair. He wanted to pull it free, to gather those lush copper waves in his hands and kiss her until she knew how much he'd missed her.

She stopped beside his chair, just barely out of reach. "Julian."

He stood, and she looked at him with eyes wilder than he remembered, and he couldn't help but smile. "You're here." He said.

Maybe he hadn't been too late after all.

Maybe he'd been just in time.

She was supposed to be in her dressing room, removing the false eyelashes and stage makeup, shedding her glittering, diamond-encrusted tutu and stepping into a blush-pink satin dress. Ivanov would be waiting, as would Chance and the crowd of ballet patrons expecting a photo, an autograph or even just a glimpse of the deaf ballerina, the star of the show. She'd become a Cinderella story.

There would be articles about her in the arts section of newspapers the next day. Probably even a full-color photograph above the fold. Come Monday, everyone in New York would know her name.

She'd done it, thanks to Julian.

He'd come. After days of silence, nights of longing for something as simple as a glimpse of his elegant hands or his lonely blue eyes, he'd been right there, in the front row. Even after that awful day in the dressing room, after everything that had gone so horribly wrong, he'd come. He'd been right there, in the front row. His had been the first face she saw when she stepped onstage.

She had to see him. Talk to him. Now, before he left and she lost her chance. The others could wait. So here they were…alone again. At last. The theater was empty. Discarded programs and empty champagne glasses littered the room.

A sob rose up Tessa's throat. This should have been the happiest night of her life. She had everything she'd always wanted. At long last, against all odds. She shouldn't have been dancing center stage tonight. She shouldn't have been the one in the spotlight. She knew as much. She should probably fall to her knees in gratitude, or at the very least, smile and pose for the balletomanes and their cameras.

Somehow, though, none of it mattered without Julian.

The moment their eyes met, Tessa forgot about the obligations waiting for her in the other room. Memories flooded her senses, screaming to be heard—Julian speaking to her with his hands, the warmth of his lyrical lips and the excruciating bliss of him moving inside her. These were the things that mattered. Nothing else.

She swallowed around the lump in her throat. She loved him. More than ballet, more than the music she still wasn't sure was real, more than the belief that she'd been caught in a wondrous, magical spell. She realized that now. She'd loved him all along.

"I wouldn't have missed this for the world. You were perfect, Tessa." He shook his head. "I'm sorry about my text. I was…"

"It's okay. You're here now," Tessa said, breathless, wanting nothing more than to touch him, to taste him, to kiss his lips as they moved into a sly hint of a smile. "You don't need to explain."

"But I do." His smile grew wider. "I played at Zander's club tonight."

"Oh, my God, that's wonderful."

It was the last thing she'd expected him to say. How was this possible? Why hadn't Zander told her?

Her brother had hinted at it, though. *You should probably check in with Julian and see what he's up to…*

He'd probably thought the news wasn't his to share. He'd also probably been trying to force them to talk to one another. Still, she was going to kill him. But first, she had something more important to take care of.

She took a deep breath and willed herself not to cry. She'd vowed that if she ever saw Julian again, she'd tell him exactly how she felt. She'd missed her chance before. She couldn't make the same mistake again.

"I love you, Julian." She smiled through her tears. "Ask me again. Please?"

He looked at her long and hard, much like the way he'd looked at her in the Bennington ballroom, when she'd asked him to take her to bed. Her heart felt like it was going to beat right out of her chest while she waited for him to respond. After several long, silent seconds, she convinced herself he was going to answer the same way he had then. *You don't know what you're saying.*

But she did know. She knew she was in love with him, and she knew she wanted to spend the rest of her life with him. They could figure out the rest along the way. They could improvise. Just like a song.

When he finally answered, he didn't use words. He used his hands...those glorious hands that Tessa loved so much. He spelled a proposal out in perfectly practiced sign language.

Will you marry me?

She made a fist with her right hand and moved it up and down. It was the sign for *yes*. Then she threw her arms around his neck and whispered it in his ear.

"Yes, I'll marry you."

For a moment, she could have sworn she heard the sound of her own voice saying yes. She was sure it was just her imagination, but maybe not. Maybe some words were simply powerful enough to make their way through the silence.

* * * * *

COMING SOON!

We really hope you enjoyed reading this book. If you're looking for more romance, be sure to head to the shops when new books are available on

Thursday 28th June

To see which titles are coming soon, please visit
millsandboon.co.uk

MILLS & BOON

Coming next month

REUNITED AT THE ALTAR
Kate Hardy

Cream roses.

Brad had bought her cream roses.

Had he remembered that had been her wedding bouquet, Abigail wondered, a posy of half a dozen cream roses they'd bought last-minute at the local florist? Or had he just decided that roses were the best flowers to make an apology and those were the first ones he'd seen? She raked a shaking hand through her hair. It might not have been the best idea to agree to have dinner with Brad tonight.

Then again, he'd said he wanted a truce for Ruby's sake, and they needed to talk.

But seeing him again had stirred up all kinds of emotions she'd thought she'd buried a long time ago. She'd told herself that she was over her ex and could move on. The problem was, Bradley Powell was still the most attractive man she'd ever met – those dark, dark eyes; the dark hair that she knew curled outrageously when it was wet; that sense of brooding about him. She'd never felt that same spark with anyone else she'd dated. She knew she hadn't been fair to the few men who'd asked her out; she really shouldn't have compared them to her first love, because how could they ever match up to him?

She could still remember the moment she'd fallen in love with Brad. She and Ruby had been revising for their English exams together in the garden, and Brad had come out to join them, wanting a break from his physics revision. Somehow he'd ended up reading Benedick's speeches while she'd read Beatrice's.

'I do love nothing in the world so well as you: is that not strange?'

She'd glanced up from her text and met his gaze, and a surge of heat had spun through her. He was looking at her as if it was the first time he'd ever seen her. As if she was the only living thing in the world apart from himself. As if the rest of the world had just melted away...

Continue reading

REUNITED AT THE ALTAR
Kate Hardy

Available next month
www.millsandboon.co.uk

LET'S TALK
Romance

For exclusive extracts, competitions
and special offers, find us online: